TWO

X

FOUR

X

MURDER

By Lorraine J. Anderson

ACKNOWLEDGEMENTS & DEDICATIONS

Thank you to Sandra Lee, Becky Lewis, and editor extraordinaire Elaine Batterby.

And, as always, the Lord, who grants all inspiration.

Dedicated to Ty, Ken, Jerrud, Jason, and all my lumber yard co-workers, present and past. None of these characters are based on you.

Table of Contents

CHAPTER 1

I stood at the door, looking into the sales office. I hadn't been here in what? Fifteen years? And yet the place hadn't changed. The sides of the counters were still covered with some sort of fake cow hide. The floor was a checkered black and red, and it looked like the demented chess board of the upcoming zombie apocalypse. If someone bled all over that floor, who would notice?

I put the scene into the back of my mind. I keep thinking that one of these days, I'm going to write a book, but it never seemed to happen. I wished that I had my notebook here, then realized that now just wasn't the time.

Maybe later on.

Then again, maybe later on, I would need a stiff drink. And another. And I don't drink.

I jerked my attention back to the office and looked around again.

The walls were covered with dark paneling; obviously paneling that no one else had wanted to buy. Behind the counter were some antique desks, the newest being from the mid-seventies. They were serviceable, but I had a feeling there was a reason they didn't make them like these anymore. The sides of the desk were green, the tops were brown. The chairs were newer — chairs did wear out after a while, after all.

On the walls were various clippings and on one wall was an obviously old map of the city of Herculaneum, Michigan. An old flier on the wall welcomed customers to Herculaneum Lumber and Building Supplies. One corner was folded over, as if no-one could be bothered to get on a stepladder and tack it back up.

A tall, large man came to the door behind me, and I moved to one side to let the customer in. None of the staff had noticed me yet, and I was glad to remain anonymous. I wouldn't be anonymous for long.

The man smiled at me and motioned me to go ahead. I motioned him up ahead of me. Unfortunately, this brought me to the attention of the men behind the counter.

The first to notice was Ted Rettig. He gave me a quick, sympathetic look, and I nodded sadly. I motioned him to wait on the man, then observed Ted.

Even though I had seen him at the funeral, I hadn't had a chance to take a good look at him. Ted had a lot more gray hair than I remembered. He was tall and thin, looking like he could use a good meal. As he leaned over to grab a book from under the counter, I noticed a shiny bald spot on the top of his head. He had a slight tic on one side of his face, and I remembered Daddy telling me that he had never wanted the top position at the lumberyard; he was content to be second.

I moved further in the office. Oh, yes. Behind the counter was Jimmy DeLeo. He recognized me too, acknowledged me with a nod, then went back to his phone call. I didn't know him as well; Ted was the one I usually saw as a child.

Another customer came in from the back door, looking grumpy. Cody Helberg came up to the counter. I didn't know him at all. He didn't make it to the funeral home visitation, and he stayed to the back of the room at the funeral.

The customer stamped his boots and brushed snow from his coat.

"Cold one," Cody said.

"Frigging cold," grumped the customer, throwing an old roofing shingle on the counter. "Damn ice broke a limb through Johnson's roof."

Cody glanced at the old shingle. "And you're going to try to shingle it in this weather?"

"Well," the man said, "I don't have a choice. It won't stick, I know, but at least they'll be happy."

"I was trying to tell Dan when he called," Ted said, "that he should just put underlayment down to protect the roof and wait until spring to fix it, but he said the owner didn't want to wait."

"His wife was fussing about how it would look and what the neighbors would think," Dan said. "You know these women..." He looked around, saw me, and closed his mouth.

I nodded and wandered down the aisle. I didn't want to bring attention to myself. I was raised around this yard, yet I didn't know anything about product application. I was an office type of person.

He shrugged. "I'll just put more nails in the shingles and hope they don't blow off."

I hoped they didn't, either. After all, if I was going to end up running this place, this was something I was going to have to deal with.

I shivered.

How did I end up here? Well, for one thing, I was my father's only child. My Dad had inherited this place from his father, who had built up a booming coal business and lumber yard. They had done a brisk business in the World War II years, when soldiers got loans and were able to afford homes.

My Dad took it over in the mid-seventies. It lasted through the recession of the early eighties, and Dad was able to keep it going until he passed away last week of a sudden heart attack.

I felt tears threaten to flow over onto my cheeks and kept them back with an effort. I would cry later.

He was three years until retirement.

I sighed and looked at hammers.

Why was I here?

Dan, the contractor at the counter, finally left. I approached the counter calmly, but my insides were quaking.

9

"Carrie," Ted said. "How are you doing?"

"Well," I said, "we're all tired, of course, but everything is over."

"It was a nice funeral," Jimmy said, uncomfortably, I thought. "Your Dad looked real good."

He was dead, I thought. Everything else was just makeup. Why do people say that?

I wished that my Mom could have come in with me. That would make the next thing I said so much easier. But Mom said that she couldn't have made herself come in, he was in every board, in every nook and cranny — her words. I suspected, knowing her, that this state wouldn't last long, but I knew their love was real. I couldn't deny that.

I reminded myself that I wasn't a gawky teenager, I was forty-three, and I had had a somewhat successful career in bookkeeping. It wasn't anything I had wanted to get into, but somehow my English Major hadn't translated into many jobs.

I took a deep breath. "We read my father's will yesterday." I stopped, looking at their faces. Ted was resigned, Jimmy's face was blank, and Cody looked a bit apprehensive.

"His wish was that the lumberyard stay open—" I saw various states of relief "—and he wanted me to be president."

Silence. I saw the three look at each other with raised eyebrows.

"I have thought long and hard about this," I said slowly. Actually, my reaction was more "What?" and "Was he crazy?" until the lawyer assured me that no, my dad hadn't been nuts and he truly had wanted me to take over. Then came the crying and the denial. Mom wasn't any help; she said that he had always believed I could do this, and, in a remarkably calm moment, said that she thought so too.

I realized they were waiting for the rest of my

sentence. "I have decided to take on the challenge."

Ted, bless his heart, smiled at me. "Your father had great hopes for you," he said. "I believe you can do this, too."

"How much do you know about lumber?" Cody said.

"Not much," I admitted. "I'm trusting you will help me with that. I will take over the bookkeeping." After working in an accounting office, I believed that there wasn't much I needed to learn about the company books. I looked around. "Where are your computers?"

The guys laughed. "What computers?" Cody said, with a grin.

"You — you must be kidding." I looked back at Dad's office. "You're keeping the records in… books?"

"Well, we do have an old computer in the back that keeps the accounts receivable," Ted said.

"You don't do the bookkeeping on it?"

"No," Ted said. "Why would we need that?"

"No internet?"

Cody grinned. "Are you kidding? Around here?"

"But — but —" I couldn't believe I didn't know this. I guess I hadn't wanted to ask. "Everybody uses computers. I'm surprised your vendors haven't insisted."

"I've been taking some things home," Cody said. He shrugged. "Our vendors understand."

Yeah, I bet. I sighed. "Do you also use fountain pens and ink wells?"

"Well," Ted said, with a grin, "we have bottles of ink upstairs." He was enjoying this way too much.

I closed my eyes and exhaled loudly.

"I think," Ted said, "our first order of business is to give you a tour of the yard."

I looked down at my clothing. I had worn the business clothes I usually wore for work — stylish slacks, low heels, and a nice shirt. I hadn't thought to dress down

11

for the yard, which was across a set of railroad tracks and had nine large buildings full of building supplies. And, as I remember, the yard covered over four acres, so even in the golf carts they – we! – use to get around the yard, I would still rather be in jeans. "I think that should wait until tomorrow," I said, apologetically. "Ted, perhaps you can help me back in the office?"

"Of course," Ted said. He glanced at the other two as if warning them. "Come back with me."

He led me down the aisle to the office and motioned me into my father's chair. I sat down, trying not to feel like a little girl. He took the other chair. "Forgive me for asking this, but did he want to keep the yard open so your Mom could have an income?"

"Partly," I admitted. "He had also included a private letter. It was almost as if he knew he was going to die early."

"He always knew that it was a possibility," Ted said. "He admitted to me that he had looked at my wife's situation, and this reminded him of the fragility of life."

What could I say? "How is Marie?"

He looked sad. "Getting worse." He left it there. I knew she had been sick for years.

"If you ever need to leave..."

"The church people come in a couple of times a day," he said, "and I go home for lunch and make sure she's eating."

"I'm sorry."

He smiled at me. "Nothing to be sorry about. I married her for better and for worse." His fingers twirled a pen automatically. "Now," he said, obviously changing the subject. "Where can we start?"

I looked at the file cabinets. I supposed the books were in there. He nodded and started pulling books out.

An hour later, I was staring at financial statements. "You hand-write financial statements? Really?"

12

Ted shrugged. "How else would we do it?"

"Nobody's encouraged you to get a computer?"

He snorted. "Besides Cody? He's all of the time telling us about the wonders of computers."

I was beginning to like young Cody.

"Well," I said, "it was a start." I pushed my blonde hair back from my forehead.

Suddenly, I heard a commotion in the sales office. "What kind of lumber are you selling here?!" a man yelled. Ted winced.

"Tell me they're joking around." I peered around the corner of the office.

A look of distaste came over Ted's face. "Sadly, no." He sat back down in the chair. "That would be Richard Nathan. He never finds anything to please him."

I shook my head. "Then why does he shop here?"

"I think he thinks we're going to cave in and give him free stuff if he complains."

"You could always kick him out."

Ted looked slightly shocked. "But he pays his bill."

"Where's John?"

I winced. John was my father's name. I could hear boot steps come back to the office. I closed my eyes, steeled myself and stood up. Ted stood in front of me. "I can handle it," I said, quietly and confidently, although I didn't feel confident at all.

"John!"

I moved forward and stuck out my hand. Richard looked at it like it was a snake, then moved his tiny brown eyes to my face. I was glad he didn't stop at my bosom.

And what did he see? A small lady, five foot four, blonde hair turning to silver, business suit. Green eyes. Hopefully a confident look on my face. "I'm Carrie Burton. Pleased to meet you."

"Carrie Burton?" He looked puzzled. And angry. "Where's John?"

Ted rolled his eyes. "Dick, where were you last week?"

"I was out of town. Hunting."

"My father passed away last week," I said, grateful that my voice wasn't shaking.

"Oh," Richard said. He frowned slightly. "So—is the yard going to be sold?"

I have to admit, after dozens of people expressing their sympathy, his reaction was a bit refreshing. Not that it made him any more likable; I was just tired of people saying how sorry they were. "No. It's not."

"Carrie is the new president," Ted said.

"Ah. Too bad."

I narrowed my eyes. I wasn't sure whether he was commenting on me being the president, my father dying, or the lumberyard not being sold. "I understand you have a problem with the quality of our lumber?" I said.

"That last bunch was full of knots."

"I believe," Ted stared at me, "that you bought our number four boards, which, since it's cheaper, would have a lot of knots in it."

I knew that was for my benefit, and I nodded at Ted, gratefully.

"So?"

Witty repartee. Oy.

"You always have the option of returning them," I said.

He gave a long-suffering sigh, and his hair flopped on his forehead. I noticed it was dirty. "No, I'll keep them. I just wanted to let you know about it."

I'll bet. I knew his type. He just wanted to complain just to hear himself complain. Some people are like that. In one of my first jobs, I had taken complaint calls. Not my favorite thing to do.

I held out my hand again, then took it back. "Thank you for letting us know. I'll look into it."

14

"Yeah," he said under his breath. "I bet." He shambled up to the front of the store, then out of the door.

You know, he would make a great villain for my imaginary book. The seemingly dumb schemer who looked like a country hick, but masterminded the hacking of the FBI's computers, meanwhile kidnapping the president, who looked a lot like Harrison Ford...

Never mind. No one would believe it.

Ted's eyes were blazing. "Shi... Swine."

I smiled slightly. "I can think of more colorful terms."

"It's ingrained. I don't swear in front of ladies."

I smiled. "I appreciate that. You know my Mother's thoughts about swear words."

"John told me. Then we both laughed."

I gave him a puzzled smile.

"Because you should have heard him back here in this office."

"Ah." I motioned back towards the books. "I suppose we had better...?"

Ted sighed.

Much later, we stood up. I had inspected the books. While I'm not a CPA — far from it — I could see that everything was neat and in order. I should probably get our CPA down here to look even closer, but the thought scared me. We were making a profit, and the last 1120 reflected that. Dad's last bonus was a lot smaller than previous years — giving oneself a bonus was a good way to reduce corporate taxes — so I knew that profits were down in the present economy.

I sighed. But the books weren't nearly as bad as I thought they might be. I loved my father, but I knew that he was trained in management, even though he was a fair to middling bookkeeper.

The handwriting had changed to my Dad's almost four years ago; that must have been when Roma, our previous bookkeeper, had passed away. I vaguely remembered that. I hadn't known her. I was off in Detroit trying to make a living.

"What do you think?" Ted said.

"I think that things aren't as bad as people keep saying."

"The good Lord knows that things are bad enough," Ted sighed. "I just hate to see the state the lumberyard has fallen into."

I regarded Ted. "We can't stay in the past," I said, even though I wanted desperately for my father to be in this chair. "We have to think of the future." Easier said than done, but I knew Ted needed to hear that.

He smiled at me. "I think you've inherited a little of your father's Blarney."

I snorted. "If I had my Dad's talent, I would have been married a long time ago." Sadly, true. I tended to speak my mind, especially around men. I never have learned the fine art of handling men. I didn't believe in speaking to their vanity.

All of which didn't endear me with my former fiancé. I shivered. Yet another reason I moved back from Detroit and didn't leave a forwarding address. That fiancé I had turned out to be a psycho.

"You did a good job with Richard Nathan."

I shrugged. "I wasn't going to be bullied my first day on the job."

He reached into his pocket and pulled out a worn stone. He handed it to me. It was a worry stone — a well-worn worry stone. "Your Dad gave this to me my first day on the job."

I looked at it. It was the deepest black I had ever seen —the depression was well worn. I rubbed it between my finger and thumb. It was oddly comforting, and I smiled. Then I handed it back.

Ted smiled and pushed my hand back, folding my

16

fingers over the stone. "Keep that. You may need it."

"Hey, squire!"

The sudden voice startled me and I bounced in my chair. Ted turned around. "Hi, Joe. How's it going today?"

"Oh, not so good, not so good." An elderly white man shuffled up. He was carrying a dirty bag, and his coat and slacks were ripped in various places. His hair was sticking straight up. While I couldn't smell anything yet— oh, yes, there it was. Unwashed body. "Ain't got nothin' today." He held a newspaper up. "You want a paper today, squire?"

"Yeah," Ted said, getting a coin out of his pocket. "I'll take a paper." Ted winked at me, handed the coin to Joe and took the paper. I could tell by the picture on the front that it was yesterday's.

The man peered at me. "Who's that?" he said, his voice quavering upwards.

"That's John's daughter. Carrie. She's president of this lumberyard now."

The man actually took a step back. "A woman president? Not in my day."

"Joe, it's 2003 now. It's the future."

"No, it ain't," Joe said. "It's 1945." Which, I figured, would make him in his mid-eighties. Dementia?

Ted smiled. "Whatever you say, Joe."

"You give me a ride home?" He had a home?

"Not today, Joe. Sorry."

"Okay." He looked back at me and laid a finger beside his nose. "Remember, there's gold in them thar hills."

I smiled. "Thanks, Joe. I'll remember that."

"You do that." He stared at me intently, then shuffled away, back up to the front desk. I could hear him try to cadge a ride from one of the salesmen, then one of the contractors.

Ted smiled. "You haven't met Joe Newton before?"

17

I shook my head. "I haven't been in town much since I graduated from college."

"He's just one of the town eccentrics. I'm not sure what's wrong with him, but he's been like that ever since anybody can remember."

"So, will anybody give him a ride home?"

Ted shrugged. "He'll wander off."

"Does he live anyplace?"

"He lives in a foster home. They let him out to wander during the days, since he always comes home. He doesn't really have Alzheimers, he's just a little strange in the head. I understand he takes medication."

"Cute old guy, considering."

"He's harmless," Ted said. He smiled at me. "If a bit smelly. They have a hard time getting him to take a bath."

I sighed. I saw a bunch of these kind of people in Detroit. My heart went out to them, but, for my own sanity, I learned to say a little prayer and pass them by. Not terribly Christian, I suppose, but I'm not Mother Theresa.

I put him out of my mind, then I started to look at the Accounts Receivable computer. Well, the good thing was that it wasn't connected to the Internet, so there was little chance for infection. But it was attached to a Dot Matrix printer. I couldn't believe it. A dot matrix?

I wish I had taken Joe home. That was the last time I saw him alive.

CHAPTER 2

"So," Mom said, "how was it?" She pulled a meatloaf out of the oven and set it before me. I sighed. I wasn't fond of meatloaf, and the way Mom made it was a bit too salty for my taste. I felt that I needed to swallow an ocean of water after one meal. But it was comfort food, and, more to the point, it was her comfort food. So I smiled at her and took a healthy slice.

"It was... interesting," I said. "I spent the day looking through the books."

Mom was jittering back and forth from the counter to the table, her hard soled shoes tapping on the floor like an overactive woodpecker. Tap tap tap tap tap. Five steps to the counter. Tap tap tap tap tap. Five steps back. "Why would you need to do that, dear?"

"If I'm going to run that place, I need to know what makes it tick." I placed a piece of meatloaf in my mouth, and my mouth just about shriveled up and tasted like a salt mine. I rapidly took a drink of water. I attacked the green beans, instead.

Mom frowned. "Ted can run it. I was hoping that you would..."

What, Mom. Stay home all day, watching you knit? "You know Daddy wanted me to work. And I thought you wanted me to take over?"

"I do. I did. I just..." She wandered around the kitchen. She finally tapped over to the kitchen table and sat down with a sigh. Sighing again, she cut herself a neat slice of meatloaf, then daintily took a bite. She chewed for a moment, then reached rapidly for the water. "Why didn't you *tell* me that I put too much salt in?"

I giggled. That was the wrong thing to do. Mom glared at me, and I sobered rapidly. A small tear slid down her cheek. "Mom, I didn't want to upset you. I know you're under a lot of stress."

"I'll be fine," she said, although it was becoming increasingly apparent that she wasn't.

"Why don't I just cook a couple of hamburgers?" I said, helplessly.

She waved her hand listlessly. I got up, pulled a fry pan out, and started cooking while Mom sat in her chair, crying. I pulled the tissues out of the nook in the wall and pushed them at her, pulling two out and placing them in her hands. Then I leaned down and gave her a hug and stayed there a couple of minutes.

She gradually stopped.

"I'm sorry, honey," she said, blowing her nose delicately. She started to get up, and I gently pushed her back down.

"I may not be the world's greatest cook," I said, "but I can at least cook a couple of hamburgers."

"Sometimes," she smiled.

"Sometimes," I agreed, and I moved back to the pan. "Like I said, I looked at the books. The lumberyard is actually doing pretty well."

Even though I had my back to her, I could hear her frown. "Daddy always said that the yard was doing lousy."

"Yes," I agreed, "compared to previous years." I turned the burgers over and turned to look at her. "But we are not losing money. Daddy was an alarmist."

"No," Mom said. "Daddy was a conservative." There was a defensive note to her voice, and, once again, I wondered how I got to be the daughter of a conservative businessman and a wannabe socialite. On the other hand, looking at some of the businessmen, they seemed to be attracted to socialites. The difference was that most of those guys changed wives with the seasons of the year.

"That he was," I said, agreeing. I cooked the hamburgers through, then brought them over to the table, snagging the ketchup and the mustard on the way by.

Mom was tracing her red nails on the table. "He thoroughly believed that the country was going to hell in a hand basket."

I loved my Daddy, but I tended towards more liberal views. "I know that's what he believed. I think, though, the country is going to turn around, like it always has." I pushed the delicately printed plates towards her. "Eat."

Mom's blood sugar always had dropped in times of stress. She cut a piece dutifully off the burger, then pushed it around her plate.

I picked up the piece of burger with my fork and pushed it toward her mouth. "Eat. You'll feel better."

"I don't want to feel better."

"Yes, you do," I insisted. "Do you want me to feed you?"

She smiled. "No." She started eating in earnest, if slowly. I observed her, covertly.

Mom looked younger than her actual age of sixty-five. Her sandy brown hair was permed into a gentle wave and fell to her shoulders. She wore a necklace of pearls — Dad's gift — and today, she was dressed in a mint green top with puffy sleeves. She was in black polyester slacks, and she wore low-slung hard soled heels. I'm not sure what style she was wearing — it certainly wasn't today's styles, it looked like it was stopped in the mid-eighties. But it fit her.

Of course, she wore makeup. Unlike her clothes, her makeup was understated — just a bit of foundation to even out her skin, and a pale lipstick and some eyeliner. I very rarely wore makeup, myself, but I could appreciate those who did.

The only place her age betrayed her was under her chin and her hands. They were starting to look like elderly lady hands. But for someone who had never had any cosmetic operations, she looked good.

She smiled at me. "You're right, darling, I do feel

better."

I nodded. "I knew you would."

The phone rang. Mom got up. "I'll get it." She picked up the phone, then frowned. "Why no, Vince, Carrie's not here. Why would she be here? She went back to Detroit." She looked worried at me.

Oh, God. Vince. My creepy ex-fiancé.

"She left today, yes." Mom acted like she was shuffling papers. "I — don't seem to have her cell phone number here. You know, with the funeral and all... Yes, thank you. Yeah, I'll take your number." She didn't make a move toward the paper. "Yes, Vince, I have it. I'll have her call the next time I see her. Goodbye." She hung up the phone. Mom stared at me. "What did you ever see in him?"

I sighed. "He looked at me."

She rolled her eyes. "You know, you should raise your standards."

"Well, he was better than some factory workers that came into the office I usually see. The good ones are married. Usually, the rest have to be reminded to take showers and brush their teeth."

"Factory workers," she mused. "You should have gone to church. Maybe you would have met somebody there."

"As I said, the good ones are married." And besides, I hadn't been to church in years, not that I'd admit that to her. I looked down. I guess we were through with supper. I got up, picked up the plates, rinsed them off, and put them in the dishwasher. Mom joined me, being very careful of her nails.

"Still," she said, "there's something wrong with Vince."

"I know, Mom." He seemed fine at first. He gave me flowers. He took me to chick flicks. He seemed to dote on me. But then he started to separate me from my friends, saying how he didn't like one or another. I laughed at him

22

at first, but gradually I realized that he was dead serious. I started reading up on men like Vince, then started withdrawing from him. What was his next step? Hitting me? Threatening me? He had already tried the last, telling me that he was going to stop seeing me if I didn't spend all of my free time with him.

As if.

It hadn't come down to the point where I had to get a restraining order on him, but I had gotten a call from him every day for a month. The last call he had threatened suicide if I didn't make up with him. This was the day I had learned my Dad had his fatal heart attack.

Like I was going to miss my last moments with my Dad to spend time with a guy who threatened suicide. I knew what he was by then; I hadn't believed him for a moment.

What a sad creature.

"Mom, we need caller ID."

She hesitated and looked at the phone. I had told her all of what I had been going through with Vince. "I have to say I agree. I'll call the phone company tomorrow to see if we can get it here. Then we won't have to take a phone call from Vince again."

I hoped Vince wouldn't think about changing phones. "Well, it will help, I think."

After dinner, Mom went into the family room and turned on the TV, and I grabbed the latest Charlaine Harris book. Somehow, reading about Sookie Stackhouse's vampire problems made mine easier to bear. I was quite glad I didn't need to deal with broody vampires.

I read until I couldn't think anymore. It was easier that way. If I started thinking, I started thinking about Vince. Or about Dad. Or about the lumberyard. Or about...

I woke up the next morning, not entirely sure how I got into bed. I stretched, looked at the ceiling of my room...

Then groaned. I had forgotten I was home. With my

mother. And *why* I was home. A couple of tears leaked out from under my eyelids, then I got up. I looked over at the clock. It was eight o'clock.

Oh, great. I was late going to my own company.

I went downstairs into the kitchen. Mom was at the counter, looking flawless as always, dressed in a fitted top and a stylish pair of slacks, handing me a bowl for cereal. She then got out a couple of cups for coffee. "Mom," I said. "Why didn't you get me up?"

She looked slightly surprised. "We have an appointment with Patricia this morning. You knew that."

"Oh. Yeah." I had forgotten. I had even told Ted about it yesterday. Patricia Dayton was our CPA. She was going to advise us what we should do with the company. Should we keep it a C-Corporation or convert it to an S-Corporation?

Exciting stuff, I thought.

Bleh.

I was a bookkeeper, I knew what I was doing, but I needed help with the overall view. I'll admit that; bookkeeping was a job, but I had always wanted to write a book.

One of these days, I'll do that.

I ate my cereal automatically while Mom did her morning crossword puzzle. I looked off into the distance while trying to plot a spy story, and somehow, Pierce Brosnan came to mind.

So, Brosnan was captured and was in the bowels of a ship, in chains...

I had a slight daydream of Brosnan in chains.

"Carrie."

I was admiring Brosnan up and down. His pectoral muscles gleamed. Somehow, he had lost his shirt...

"Carrie!"

I shook my head and looked at my Mom.

"Who's a famous doctor turned wordsmith?"

She had interrupted me for a crossword puzzle clue? I closed my eyes. "Roget."

"Oh. Yeah." She filled in the word.

I scraped the bottom of my bowl. "Was that it?"

She seemed to be surprised. "Well, no," she said, surprising me. I was expecting her to say yes. "I think your Father thought he would die young," she said, her eyes down.

I blinked, surprised at my Mom. The last time I was home, two months ago, he seemed healthy and hale. He had encouraged me on my job hunt; because he saw that I was discouraged being on unemployment. He told me he knew I could do it, and he hadn't breathed a word about his will.

In retrospect, I'm surprised he hadn't offered me a job. Perhaps because he knew I wouldn't take it. I respected my Father too much to work with him.

So now I was supposed to take his job.

Ack.

"Mom, I'm not so sure I can step into Daddy's shoes. I'd be happy to be a bookkeeper for a new President, but I don't think I'm leadership material."

Mom had turned back to her puzzle. "Bullshit."

I gaped. Mom never swore. "What did you say?"

"Bullshit. You can do it. I saw it, and your Father knew it. He thought you were wasted in that little bookkeeping job."

"He never said anything."

"No. He wouldn't. You know that he wanted you to go into accounting in the first place."

I sighed and nodded. I fought him every step of the way. I had wanted to be a teacher; he argued that I should be a CPA. I hated bookkeeping. I won. In college, anyway. When I got through my student teaching, I found that I had actually hated teaching, although I loved individual students. I could have gone into teaching, I suppose, but instead I found a job in an office, doing data input. Barbara

Katon, my immediate boss, took me under her wing and slowly but gradually taught me everything I knew about bookkeeping.

Funny how life works.

"Look," Mom continued, "I just want you to try. I would rather keep it in the family then turn it over to some stranger."

I smiled. "Ted Rettig is not a stranger."

"And he's been very vocal about not being the President." She smiled sadly. "I agree with him. Besides, he's almost as old as your dad. He's going to retire in the next couple of years. Which makes him ideal to be your mentor."

I stared at my Mother. She was turning me upside down. I had never thought she knew so much about business.

She laughed at my expression and laid her pen down. Why had I never noticed that she did her crossword puzzles in pen?

"Mom? Why didn't you ever work out of the house?"

"Because," she said, "your father could be very reclusive. I knew that in order to make the business a success, he would need to move a little in social circles. So, I did the social thing, bringing him along when I could, and I kept house and raised you." She smiled. "I never regretted it. And we didn't need the money."

That was my next question.

There didn't seem to be much else to say. I picked up my bowl, rinsed it out, and put it in the dishwasher. "Mom?"

She had already turned back to her puzzle.

"Why don't you sell the yard?"

She looked thoughtful, then sad. "Because — I know that Daddy wouldn't want me to."

"And if it turns out that it's the best thing to do?"

She turned back to her puzzle. "We'll take that step when we need to." She filled in another line. "I have had an offer already." She shivered. "Something about that Mike Collinsworth gives me the creeps. His hair is greasy, for one thing, and I always expect to see the grease on his shoulders."

I snorted. My mom tended to exaggerate. "When is our appointment?" I said, changing the subject.

"Ten O'clock."

I went upstairs to take a shower and dress. When I came down, Mom was in the front room, starting to put on her coat. I looked at the clock. "Aren't we a little early?"

"You need to pick up the books, don't you?"

"You take the books to the CPA?"

She shrugged. "Of course. How else would you do it?"

"Well, if we had computers..."

"Which you don't. So, we pick up the books."

The drive was silent. I pulled up in front of the lumberyard and walked in the front door. The guys stared at me, then went back to their work. I walked back to where Ted was looking through some invoices. "Hi, Carrie."

"Just picking up the books," I said.

He got up and unlocked the cabinet. "I hope you have a successful meeting." He actually looked a little apprehensive.

"What's wrong?"

He exhaled through his nose, then closed the door. "Are you going to sell the lumberyard?"

I shut my eyes. "I said I wasn't. You know that. And my Mom doesn't want to."

"Yes, but what your Mom wants and what's practical is two different things. I just want you to know that we'll all understand if you decided to sell." He sighed. "We all talked this morning."

I set the books down. They were getting heavy. All

27

the more reason to introduce the twenty-first century to this place — even diskettes would be much easier to carry. "She's convinced me to try to do the President job. She'll keep it open at least that long." I smiled and lowered my voice. "I'm not sure I can do it, but I'm not going to let Mom down."

"Good," he said. He seemed to relax slightly.

"She's hoping you will be my mentor."

He relaxed even further. "I'd be proud to."

"I know you've said you don't want the job, but I'm surprised that you're not mad you weren't even offered the job."

"Oh," he smiled, "your Dad offered me the job a long time ago."

"Yeah?" I blinked. "While he was still running it?"

"Well, the conversation was hypothetical," he explained. "But I think my reaction was what sealed his thoughts. I encouraged him to go with his original thought, which was you."

How long had he been thinking about it?

I must have shown some of this on my face, because he smiled slightly. "He's been thinking about it ever since you graduated from college and got that bookkeeping job."

I snorted. "You know, it's not like I've been taking the biggest career track to success."

"No," Ted said. "But at least it was in business. I'm not sure what he would have done had you gone into, say, copy editing. I think he would have been proud of you, regardless."

I picked up the books again. "I still can't believe that he's gone."

Ted winced. "Me, neither."

I carried the books through the showroom. Ted held the door. "The books are going to leave the office?" Cody said.

I smiled at him. "I'm surprised the books don't turn into dust when they cross the threshold," I said back.

Cody snorted.

I placed them carefully in the back seat of the car. "Any problems?" Mom said.

"No," I said. "I was just having a couple of words with Ted."

"Too bad he can't come along." Mom commented.

That had never occurred to me. "Why couldn't he?"

"I asked. He didn't want to."

"Ah."

I drove carefully to Patricia's office and carried the books into the office. "Hi," the lady said behind the counter. "You must be Carrie."

I had been here once before, but I didn't know this person. She was tall, thin, had poufy big hair, and her perfume was just about ready to make me sneeze. It smelled like a Rose garden—and I was allergic to roses. "I am," I said, trying hard not to sniff.

"I'm Kara Champion." She held out her hand, realized what she was doing, then offered the counter for the books. "I'll let Patricia know that you're here." She swayed back to the office. I glanced at Mom; she was blinking rapidly. She was just as allergic to roses as I am.

Patricia popped out of the office behind Kara. "Hi," she said. "Hello, Marie. I was so sorry to hear about John. I'm sorry I didn't make it to the funeral."

Marie clasped her hand. "It's been a tough few days. I didn't even notice you were missing."

"A few people?"

"Seemed like tons, to me." I said. "I hadn't realized that my father was so popular."

Patricia seemed genuinely regretful. "He was a good man." She took the books from me. "I've been trying to get him to get computers for a couple of years now."

"Only a couple of years?" I said. "Personal

computers have been around for a long time."

"Well," she shrugged. "I knew he wasn't going to agree, so I didn't waste my words."

Mom smiled. "I've thought he should get computers for years. But I think he was a little afraid of them."

"What," I said. "Like they were going to sprout legs and teeth and attack him?"

"No, he was afraid that he would lose all of the data," Mom said. "He said, at least with books, they're permanent."

"Yeah," I snorted. "Until the next fire took out the office and the file cabinet they were stored in."

"Still," Patricia said, "this is what we have." She led us to the office, and we sat down. She made a click on her computer — starting her time, I suppose — then looked at us. "What would you like to know?"

I looked at Mom, and she gave me the go-ahead gesture. "My father wanted me to take over as President in the event of his death. I've looked over his books, and I believe we're still making a profit. Now—the first thing is to take care of my mother. What would you recommend?"

After a few minutes, I sat back. It was just as I thought. The company was in good shape. Barring disaster, Mom was good for the rest of her life. I relaxed.

"Now," Patricia said. "There's the matter of electing you as officer. Your board will have to do that."

I blinked. "Who's on the board? And how big could this be?"

"Your Dad, of course." Patricia pulled something up on the computer. "Ted." She looked at the screen again. "Oh, James DeLeo."

"Jimmy? Really?"

"He's one of the original stockholders."

I hadn't talked to Jimmy in years, and we hadn't had much chance to talk the other day. "Who else?"

"A couple of others. Unfortunately, if they're all

against you, they can vote you out as President."

"Then I had better talk to them, hadn't I?" Mom said.

"No, Mom," I said. "I should talk to them." I thought of something. "Is there any reason any of them would vote against me?"

"Apart from Jimmy being a chauvinist pig?" she said, innocently. "No, no reason in the world."

Thanks, Dad.

"Still," Patricia interjected, "you are still majority stockholders, so it would be very difficult to remove you. But they could make your life hell."

I rolled my eyes. Wonderful.

"Like I said," Mom said. "I'll talk to them."

Why did that feel like a bad idea?

CHAPTER 3

I walked into the lumberyard the next day a little before 7:00 A.M., toting my mug of extra strong coffee. The crew was still standing at the front desk, waiting for starting time. The good-natured laughing went silent as I walked in.

"May I help you?" said a young black man, while looking at the other men.

Jimmy snorted. "That's our new president, jughead."

I stuck my hand out. "I'm Carrie Burton."

He looked at my hand. I could almost feel the embarrassed heat coming from him. "I'm Matthew Weist. I'm one of the drivers."

"I don't bite," I said.

He took my hand gingerly. "I'm sorry I mistook you for a customer."

"I'm not," I said. "Shows you have initiative." And it did. I knew that this company had a tradition of bringing in office employees from the yard; maybe he would be a good candidate.

Jimmy snorted. "I think he's just sucking up to the boss."

I stared at Jimmy. "He didn't know me," I said with a crooked smile. "I didn't expect any of the rest of you to get up."

Ted smiled. "Except to get up for a lady."

It was my turn to snort. "If I'm working here, I had better unlearn being a lady."

"Just stay around here," Cody laughed. "We'll teach you soon enough."

I smiled. "I'm going to want to talk to all of you later on." I could see some faces fall. "I just want to get to know you. If we're going to be working together, I think that's important, don't you?"

I could see some reluctant nods and some looks amongst themselves. I just wanted to talk. Honestly, you would think I had asked them to take up knitting.

I was beginning to see what an uphill battle that being a woman in the lumberyard world will be.

They looked up at the clock. Time to start work. Mathew took a can that looked like it was full of keys. I looked at Ted. "Opens up the buildings out back." Of course.

"Come on, Tiny, get your ass out of the chair," Sam said to Cody.

Cody grinned at Sam. "You first, Snuffy."

Tiny? Snuffy? Who were these guys, the seven dwarves? I raised my eyebrows. "Ted, can I see you?"

"Of course," Ted said. He motioned to the guys to start working.

I sat behind the desk, still feeling very much like a little girl sitting at the big kid's table. "Ted," I said quietly. "Can I use you as a touchstone? I've worked in an office with mostly women. This is a bit different."

He looked thoughtful. "Yes. It would be. Roma found a balance, but, then again, she wasn't expected to wait on customers or be a supervisor."

I nodded ruefully. "I can't be one of the guys, but yet again, I can't let them ride over me. I need to learn to be a woman in a man's world."

"May I make a suggestion?"

"Of course." I took a sip of coffee.

"You need to dress down."

I looked at my outfit. I was wearing a long sleeved, ruffled blouse, accessorized by a necklace, and wool slacks. "I thought I was dressing down."

Ted winced. "My wife would be better at this, but while I know you need to dress better than we do, you do need to wear something more in line of what the guys are wearing."

I thought about what they were wearing. "I am not wearing t-shirts to work."

"I don't expect you too. But dressing much better than they are suggests that you are better than they are. We need to maintain a team effort." He sighed. "Your Dad knew that. Do you remember what he wore to work?"

"Plain short sleeve shirts and blue jeans. Sometimes he wore black slacks or khakis." I looked at my wool slacks. "I guess I had better do some shopping." I changed the subject. "Is there anyone I should interview first?"

"I'd take Jimmy."

"Can you send him back?" Might as well get this started. I still felt a little shaky about the whole thing—I had never interviewed anybody in my life—but if my Dad thought I could do it, I was going to try.

I was so glad that I took that theater class in college and had dabbled in the community players while over at the big city. I put my calm face on and waited for Jimmy.

He walked in. Jimmy was a little older. In his youth, he had been a weightlifter, but now the only weight he lifted was his fork and his beer belly. "Miss Burton."

"Carrie, please, like you've been calling me all of my life."

He lowered himself into the chair with a groan. Too late, I realized that I should have asked him to close the door, so I got out of my chair and did it for him. His brown eyes watched me, and I had the feeling he wasn't seeing me as I am today, he was seeing the small girl that I was, asking for quarters for the machine.

"Jimmy? I'm still trying to get a handle on this company, what we may need to change, and what we need going forward." I got out a yellow pad and a pen. "What would you say that our strengths are?"

He looked at me and I could almost see his prejudice against female executives pop up. "Your Dad never

35

asked things like that."

I kept my pen poised. "Because he knew this business inside and out. If I'm going to be president, I need to learn these things fast."

"You *are* going to be president?"

I set the pen down and looked him in the eye. "My father entrusted me with the care of this company and the support of my mother." I picked up the pen again. "Yes, I'm going to be president." *If it kills me*, I said to myself, *which it might.*

That got his attention. "I still remember giving you quarters for the machine."

I grinned. "And thank you."

He took a deep breath. "Well, for one thing, we have loyal customers..."

Once the ice was broken, he gave me some invaluable insights and some not so valuable. He thought Cody was too young to be in the office, he thought Mathew was too flighty, he hated Richard Nathan, and Mike Collingsworth had approached all of them to get info about the company. There were also a few other contractors he hated, and he was about ready to retire, and he hated to be left in the office while the guys wandered around the yard.

I guess I couldn't blame him for the last.

I reflected that he was only two or three years until retirement. As I remembered, he came in from the yard himself, after thirty years of being a yard supervisor. After he ran down, I stood up. "Thank you," I said, genuinely. "I appreciate you being so open with me."

He hesitated. "Will I—keep my job?"

"Of course," I said. "As long as you want." Even if I might have to get the others to cover for him. I considered him. He was overweight and he was puffing just from the effort from talking so much. Emphysema, I thought.

"Thank you," he said, and as he looked at me, I had the feeling he knew what I was thinking.

"Can you send Cody back?"

He nodded and walked slowly to the front.

Cody Helberg was much different. He bounced in the room, and, while I'm only in my mid-forties, he made me feel like a hundred-and ten-year-old granny. He had blond hair and pale blue eyes and wire frame glasses. He reminded me of John Denver when he was with the Muppets. He was also shorter than I was. He wore a Herculaneum High School team t-shirt and nice jeans. "You wanted to see me?" he said.

"Close the door."

His eyes got wide. I smiled. "No, you're not in trouble. I just wanted to talk." Geez, was I that scary? I thought back to when I first met my old boss, Barbara Katon. She had looked at me over her reading glasses with those steely grey eyes and I had felt like fading into the wallpaper. I smiled again, trying desperately to project confidence and friendliness.

"I'm asking everybody their thoughts about the company. I'm just new here, you see..." He smiled, and I decided to take a little different tack. "And I wanted to see what ideas you have to improve the company."

That did it. First, he started off on computers, and my heart warmed to him. Why take the time to do the books by hand if a computer could do it easier? That's just drudge work.

Then, with encouraging noises from me, he started on the state of the buildings and the condition of the trucks and the quality of the lumber. I hadn't paid much attention to lumber before; I had thought a board was a board was a board. But, as I knew from Ted the other day, there were, apparently, different qualities of board and different qualities of plywood and etcetera and etcetera and so on.

Then I asked, "What do you think of our contractors?"

That started him on another subject. Most, it seems,

were good guys, with a few troublemakers in the bunch. I took notes, meaning to ask Ted later about those. Then I asked the conversation stopper. "What do you think about Mike Collingsworth?"

His face shut down. "I don't know."

I looked at him with astonishment. "Really?"

"Please don't ask me about him."

"Oh? Why?"

He swallowed. "He's... my uncle."

My mouth gaped open. "I see." I closed my mouth. If this was one of the mysteries I read, he never would have admitted his relationship. On the other hand, this was a small town, and half of it was related to the other half, by blood or by marriage. And most all of them knew each other.

I might be exaggerating, by not by much.

"Your Uncle seems to want to buy this lumberyard somehow."

Cody nodded. "He does have the money."

I looked around. "Why? I mean, I like this place and I believe that it does the city a service." I reviewed what I said and realized that I still hadn't invested myself into this place. "I mean, *we* do the city a service. What would your Uncle get out of it?" I looked at Cody's face and realized that I had put him in an awkward situation. "Sorry, you don't have to answer."

He relaxed slightly. "Thanks." He looked at me earnestly. "Miss Burton..."

"Carrie. Please."

"Carrie. Your father taught me everything I know. I just wanted to let you know that I'll try not to betray his memory."

Which is slightly different than being loyal to the company, but oh well. "I appreciate that."

"You can count on me."

I got up. "Thank you. I'd like to talk to Mathew,

next."

Cody got up and opened the door. "He's out in the yard. I'll call him up."

"Not too fast." He looked at me. "Little girl's room."

"Ah." He smiled.

As I used the bathroom, my head was whirling. I was certainly getting an education in this company today. Before my Dad had passed, I had never thought much about this place. Well, I guess I knew that it would be my problem eventually; I mean, I knew my parents couldn't last forever. I washed my hands and dabbed some water on my face. Refreshed, I grabbed a cup of coffee from the pot on the way by and went back to the office.

I looked at my notes for a second, then Mathew Weist walked in. He held out his hand. "You asked for me, Ms. Burton?"

This was the young man I had wanted to know more about. "Mathew. I read your file yesterday" — and I had, that was one thing that Ted had gone over with me — "and I was surprised that with a background like yours, you were a driver."

He smiled and shrugged. "In this economy, a man has to start somewhere."

How do I phrase this without insulting him? "But," I said slowly, "you could move to Detroit and start out in a much better job than the one here in this small company."

"My family is here," he said simply. "More importantly, my elderly grandmother is here, and I'm supporting her."

"But you could move..."

"She won't move." He smiled. "And I won't move her."

"Still..."

"Are you discouraging me from working here?"

I must have blushed a complete red. "No! I'm sorry.

It's just that I don't often see a college business graduate driving a delivery truck."

"You've lived in Detroit for a number of years, haven't you?"

"I have."

He nodded wisely. "Don't be embarrassed, I get this argument from my brothers and sister all of the time."

I smiled back. "Well, then." I looked at my notes. "I'm trying to get an idea of what this company has done and what it should do in the future. What are your thoughts?"

He looked thoughtful, and as he looked thoughtful, he looked young. I reflected that he was only around twenty-four. Still, if my Dad had hired him, I wondered if he had an agenda of eventually bringing Mathew into the office. I made a note to ask Ted later.

As we talked, I realized that while some of his thoughts were strictly textbook—as one would expect from somebody just out of school—some were quite insightful. Well. I hoped my first impression was a good one. He would be great to bring in from the yard before Ted or James retired to get some training.

"Have you worked on computers?" As soon as that had left my mouth, I know how stupid that sounded. I laughed at myself. "That was a stupid question. I'm showing my age."

He grinned back at me. "I won't hold it against you."

I snorted. "I hope not." I thought back. "Weist. Is your father's name Russell?"

He looked sad. "It was."

I raised my eyebrows. "He died?"

"Cancer. Five years ago."

I swallowed. "I'm sorry. He was my classmate. He was a good guy, and a friend of mine."

He smiled. "I know. He told me."

"I'm surprised." I wonder what he had said. I had dated him a couple of times, but then he decided he liked Cherise better. He dumped me, but he was classy about it and let me down gradually. "And your mother?"

"Car accident. Three years ago."

"Damn. You're much too young for that crap. I'm sorry."

He shrugged. I opened the door. "Thanks. I'll let you go back to work."

"Thanks for talking with me."

"My pleasure," I said. "If you find Sam Kline out there, can you send him in?"

"I'll let him know." He leaned toward me conspiratorially. "Don't be surprised if he doesn't come in right away."

I snorted silently. "I read his employment record."

I pulled out Sam's employment record again. Sam had been cited a couple of times for being late. I discounted that, knowing my Dad, one minute late according to his clock meant that someone was incredibly late. The more serious fault, in my mind, was that every once in a while he seemed to "lip off" to customers.

Well, he had better not "lip off" to me, then I realized that I was forming a judgment before I met the man. I looked again. In spite of his faults, he had worked here for ten years, and that was a plus in my book. In fact, none of the employees had been short term. Even Mathew had been here three years, and, considering he was only twenty-four and came here after college, I would have expected him to move on long before this.

I reviewed the rest of the records more thoroughly than I had yesterday. There was very little on Ted. In fact, the bulk of his records seemed to be revised W-4s, and one note on his wife. Jimmy had a little more. He had a few complaints about not moving fast enough to help customers, and a couple of complaint letters from a contractor

41

named Troy Galligan. I went to the computer and pulled up the record on Galligan. He bought quite a bit of wood here; alternatively, his record was littered with late notices. I made a disapproving noise in my throat. In my mind, if a customer was late with his payments, he wasn't that great a customer, no matter how much he bought.

On to Cody. Nothing bad, but Daddy thought that Cody was too quick to make a sale and didn't follow through on things, even though, on the other hand, he was a good salesman.

Mathew seemed to be a puzzle to Daddy. His record was spotless; on the other hand, there was one complaint letter from a Hiram Long. I looked at the letter; most of the objections seemed to be that Mathew was African-American. I shrugged.

Just for the fun of it, I looked into the file at some of the past employees. In spite of our current state of long-term employees, it seemed as if the whole town had worked here at one time. The all-time employee high seemed to be around twelve; now the company employed six. I sighed. A victim of the economy.

I looked up at the clock. A half hour had passed. If Sam Kline had intended to make any brownie points with me, this wasn't a great way to start. From my office, I could look out into the showroom. A small man slouched around the corner and walked towards me. He gave me a look, then came into the office and sat down, perching at the end of his chair like some sort of vulture.

"May I help you?" I finally said.

"I'm Sam Kline," he muttered.

Oh. I thought about asking him to get out of my office, but I needed to give the guy a chance. Didn't I? I held out my hand. "I'm Carrie Burton."

He ignored the hand. "I know."

"I thought maybe I'd see you sooner." I tried to keep the sarcasm out of my voice, but a little crept in.

"Had to unload a truck," he said to the ground. "Truck drivers won't wait."

I gave him the benefit of the doubt. I could double-check with Ted later. "I was familiarizing myself with the company and the business, and I wanted to get the employees' takes on everything." I hesitated. "For example, what would you say are the strengths of this business?"

"I dunno," he said. "It's not like I'm paid to think."

I cocked my head. "You must do some thinking," I smiled, trying to give him the benefit of the doubt. "I haven't heard bad things about your work." No, I haven't *heard* bad things, I just saw things in his file. I sat back and looked at my notepad, trying to think of a specific question I could ask him. "You've been here a while. I see from the books that the inventory levels have gone down. What do you think about the inventory levels? Do you think we have enough stock for our customers?"

His answer was short and abrupt. "No."

I waited a minute. "Can you elaborate?"

"No." He got up. "Can I get back to work?"

Do I confront him now or later? "Yes. But I will talk to you later."

He pursed his lips, then exited the office. I watched him clump out and sighed. Ted came back. "He really is a good employee," he said apologetically.

"Just a mite sensitive, huh?"

"He has an attitude."

"You think?"

"But your father was able to bring him around."

"I think that's his problem," I said. "I'm not my father."

Ted nodded. "And you're not your father's son, you're your father's daughter. That doesn't help."

"No. And I come into the company from out of nowhere. And I'm taking over." I sat back. "I'm surprised I'm not getting any more resentment."

43

"Oh," Ted said. "Your Dad has been talking about this for a long time. We all knew you would take over when he retired."

Now it was me who pursed my lips. "And you know who he didn't talk to."

"Sam? He was informed..."

"No," I said bleakly. "Me." I looked around, but I didn't see anything I could throw. I could feel my face get red.

Ted looked at my face. "You're angry."

I thought somewhat of saying "you think?", but I refrained. It wasn't Ted's fault that my Dad died of a heart attack, although it's possible this place was at fault. I pulled Ted's worry stone out of my purse, and Ted smiled. "Keep that close. You may need it."

CHAPTER 4

The next few days went by fast. I started to learn the names of the contractors and met most of them. I learned about the accounts payable from Ted, who had been taking care of it since Dad passed away. He was quite glad to get rid of the job.

And I was quite glad to take it; I was feeling a bit useless. The planned tour of the barns kept getting put off; I was just as happy. I wished it could wait until spring, but I knew it couldn't.

Finally, the next week, the weather was better. I glanced out the window. "Hey, Ted," I said. "Think we can take that tour today?"

"Beautiful day," he agreed. "I think we can."

One of our customers, Mark Austin, was out in the showroom when we suited up and went out. His big dog bounded up to me. I grinned and got a treat out of the ready container on one of our file cabinets.

I held it out. The black dog sat and smiled at me. I held out my hand, and he put his paw in mine. I gave him the treat, and he gulped it with one gulp.

Ted was waiting by the door. "Ready?"

I gave Buef another pet and headed towards the door. Ted opened it. Buef gave a yip, ran out of the door and over the railroad tracks. "Buef!" Mark said. "Get back here."

All of us chased after him. He smiled back at us and ran on, then suddenly put the brakes on and stopped by building number three. He sniffed for a minute, then disappeared in an opening under the floor.

I looked at the hole. "I'm not going in there," I said.

"Probably going after a cat," Ted said. "Or a raccoon. There's a bunch of animals that live under there."

Mark leaned over and peered in the opening. "I can

see him. Buef! Get out here!" He stood up and coughed. "Smells like cat piss under there." He leaned over again. "BUEF!"   Buef started backing out. He had something in his mouth. It didn't look like a cat. Or a raccoon. Or any sort of animal.

As he cleared the opening, he dropped his load, then he smiled up at us, his tongue hanging out.

I screamed.

It was an arm. And it was attached to a body.

I stared down at the arm. Ted got down on his hands and knees and looked into the opening. "Is he... dead?" I quavered.

"I think so." He touched the arm lightly. "He's very cold." His voice was rather shaky. Buford was still sniffing around the body, but Mark was holding him back. As Ted looked at him, he pulled Buford away. "Come on, Buef. Damn." I don't think he was swearing at Buef, I think he was looking at the body. He pulled the dog across the tracks and put him in his truck. The dog looked out the window mournfully, his breath fogging the glass.

"We need to call 911."

Ted exhaled. "Yes."

"I'll do it," I said. I needed to get away from the body. I walked as calmly as I could across the tracks, walked into the office, and went up to the telephone. Jimmy and Cody glanced at me, then stared frankly as I picked up the phone and called 911.

When the lady answered, I said. "We found a body."

I have to give the emergency services a lot of credit; she didn't miss a beat. I could see the shock in the faces in the office.

"Your address?"

"Two forty three South Main Street," I said, still un-naturally calm. "Herculaneum Lumber." I leaned on the counter. "I think he's dead."

46

I barely noticed Cody wheeling a chair behind me. He pushed me on the shoulder and I collapsed on the chair, the phone falling out of my hand. "Ma'am? Ma'am?"

Cody grabbed the phone. "I think she's in shock," he said into the phone. "No, we won't move it. Yes. Thank you." He grabbed the walkie-talkie and called out to the yard. I noticed this in the back of my mind, I hadn't realized that the company had walkie-talkies. How progressive.

Jimmy grabbed a cup of coffee and put it into my hands. "Drink."

I took a sip of coffee and almost spat it out. The coffee was overcooked. Oddly enough, it made me feel better. I looked at Jimmy.

"What's going on?" he said brusquely.

"Buef pulled a body from under number three."

I finally noticed that they both looked as shocked as I felt. "Any idea..."

"Who it was?" I finished. "No. No clue." I thought of a detail. "Except the arm looked old."

Cody wrinkled his nose. "Like he had been there a while?"

"No," I said. "Like he was elderly. And his nails were dirty. His whole arm was dirty. And he was wearing a gold class ring." Where had I seen that before?

"The dirt could have been from Buford," Jimmy said.

"No, it was worse than that." I thought a minute. "I mean, like he hadn't taken a bath in a while." I hesitated. "You know, it could have been a woman." But as I said that, I doubted it. That was a man's class ring.

"You're pretty observant," Jimmy said. "Considering you only saw it a second."

"I've practiced observing," I said abstractedly. They looked puzzled at each other. I could hear the sirens come up. We live in a small town; the police station is around the corner. "I want to do writing on my spare time."

47

"Oh, yeah?" Cody said, looking interested. "What do you write?"

"I thought about mysteries," I said, abstractedly, not realizing at the time how odd that sounded. "Oh, my God, I'm going to have to tell my Mother."

The guys didn't say anything for a second, then Cody said, "I wouldn't say anything right now."

I didn't answer. I looked out into the yard at building three. Sam Kline had walked up to the crowd. As I watched, Mathew drove in. He glanced to one side, then jumped out of the truck. He looked at the arm with as much shock as I had.

The front door opened, and a customer came in. "I think," I said in shock, "that we had better close shop today, don't you?" I said abstractedly to the guys.

They nodded. "Why?" said the tall man. He looked out the window. "What's happened?" He saw the police cars pull in over the tracks, and to barn number three. "What's going on?"

"We don't know, Al," Cody said. "I can sell you out of the showroom, but we're closing for a while."

The tall man blinked. "Is that... an arm?" he said.

I looked over the tracks. That guy had better eyesight than I did. I couldn't see it. Maybe his height gave him an advantage? "Yes," I said shortly.

He looked curiously at me. "Carrie Burton," I said.

"John's daughter?"

"Yeah."

"Al Smithson," he said. I noticed he didn't have a wedding ring on. Which didn't mean much, it could be he kept it off at work. Still, I took a closer look at him. Good looking, brown eyes, a small scar on his face and a bigger one on his fingers. "What a crappy start to your new job."

I looked out at the building. "Yeah."

He stood watching with me, then the police came across the tracks. The officer zeroed in on me. "I was told you called it in."

"Yeah," I said. "I was there when Buford..." I couldn't finish the sentence.

"Buford?" the guy said, puzzled. "Which one of you is Buford?"

The guys smiled. I got up and went to the door, pointing out at Mark's truck. "That's Buford."

The big black dog smiled out at the police officer and barked.

"Ah." He snorted. "I guess I can't ask him where the body was originally."

I shrugged.

"Do you know who it is?" I asked. I sincerely hoped it was nobody I knew. Suddenly, I realized who it was, and the blood drained from my face. "It's Old Joe," I gasped.

Everybody looked at me curiously. Cole looked more than a little bit suspicious. "How do you know that?"

I blinked. "The ring." I said.

"Ring?"

"On his hand? I noticed it the other day when he was trying to get a ride from Ted. It was turned backward on his hand, and I thought, oh, how odd."

"You know Joe?"

"I saw him the other day. He asked Ted for a ride."

"Yeah, I guess old Squire won't be doing that anymore," the officer said.

"That seems rather cold," I said, peering at his ID, "Officer Cole."

He ducked his head. "Hey, I liked old Squire. He never gave us any problem. Only problems we had with him were with the people who thought he was dangerous. Hell, he wasn't dangerous, except maybe to himself."

"Then why would somebody want to kill him?" I said. I looked startled at what came out of my mouth. Why did I assume that someone killed him? I guess because I didn't figure he crawled under barn three by himself. The

49

man I saw could barely walk, much less get on his hands and knees.

"Why do you think someone killed him?" said the officer, his face darkening. I could see the thought on his face — she knew the body, and she just suggested that he was killed.

"Hey," I said. "I just moved into town. Why would I want to kill an old man?"

"Give her a break," Al said.

"And what are you doing here?" Officer Cole said, his face still dark.

Al raised his hands. "Hey, I came in for some wood," he protested. "I just walked in before you did."

The Officer's walkie-talkie crackled. "714 to 640."

"640," he said, into the microphone.

"We need you back out here. Bring your witness."

"Ten-four." He turned back to me. I was already shrugging my coat back on.

"I heard," I said. The last thing I wanted to do was look at that dead body again. "I'm coming." I pretended that this was a TV show, but as I hit the cold air, I had a hard time pretending that.

We walked silently across the tracks. The closer we got, I realized what had attracted Buford to that spot. Now that the body was out into the open, I could smell it. There was an odor of decay, an odor of unwashed body, and an odor of feces and urine. It was hard to tell whether the urine was from the body or not. I swallowed hard and told myself not to gag or throw up.

That was the hardest thing I ever did, other than telling myself not to bawl like a baby at Daddy's funeral.

I exhaled. It didn't help with the stench, but it helped me. I looked down at the hand. It was sitting palm up, and the body was lying against the opening. The palm was soft and slightly wrinkled. The class ring I had noticed was on backwards, which was probably why I had noticed it. The sleeve of his winter coat was pulled half-way up his sleeve, and the arm and wrist were slightly sunken in. It was cut, and I didn't think that was from the dog, simply because it looked like the wounds had bled, and I knew a body didn't bleed after a person was dead.

My curiosity overcame my revulsion, and I leaned over to look into the opening. His face was turned the other direction, which was a blessing. I could see more openings in the coat, but I couldn't tell if they were new cuts or old. I could also see that something had been nibbling on his arm, and I swallowed hard. Well, the guys had said that there were raccoons and cats under this building; it goes to prove that there were also mice and rats. I swallowed again.

"Do they know anything yet?" I whispered to Ted.

"I don't think so," Ted said. "They're still looking for clues."

"What I don't understand," I said, looking at the small opening, "is how he got in there."

"Oh," Ted said, looking thoughtful. "They haven't asked about that yet. I'll have to tell — "

Just then, another officer walked up.

"So," I said to him, looking at the yellow tape being strung up, "you think he was murdered?"

"Interesting first words." The officer blinked and looked innocent. "Let's do introductions first. I'm Detective Stetson Reed."

Stetson? I thought.

He held out his hand. "I'm Carrie Burton," I said, handing out my hand. "I'm — President and CEO."

He glanced at Ted, as if to confirm my statements. I couldn't blame him; I barely could believe it myself. He nodded slightly.

"I'm sorry to hear about your father."

"Thank you."

"I understand that you called in the report."

"Yes," I shrugged. "Somebody had to call it in, and

51

since I was the most freaked out—" Officer Reed smiled "—I was elected."

"Stetson," Ted said. "I wanted to point something out before I forget."

"Yes, Mr. Rettig?"

Ted smiled. "You're not in my Scout troop anymore. Call me Ted."

"My Mom would kill me," Officer Reed said. "Anyway, you were saying?"

"I'm not sure how the body was placed under the building," he said. "But I wasn't sure you were aware there was a trap door in the floor."

"Where?"

Ted moved to the front of the building and up a couple of steps. Curious, I followed.

Ted pointed. "There."

The floor of the building was ancient. It looked like it would collapse if anyone stepped onto it. I looked around. This building contained wooden trim and various other items, including a table saw — presumably to cut the trim. The trap door was no more than a square of wood, set with a finger pull on one end.

"What is that used for?" Reed said.

Ted shrugged. "I don't know. That was long before my time. It just leads to a dirt floor, now."

I looked closer at it. Yes, it looked like the dirt was disturbed, even though there were horizontal marks, like someone had tried to sweep the floor. If this was an attempt to cover up their tracks, it was pretty lame.

"I don't see where it was disturbed."

He didn't? I pointed. "That floor's been swept."

Reed leaned down and stared at the floor. I was wondering how obvious the clue had to be before Reed actually noticed it. Ted looked, too. "It could be, too," Reed said slowly, "that it was just swept."

"Just in that spot?" I said. "And why didn't they

sweep up the shavings over by the saw?"

Reed got an odd look on his face. "You're right."

"Can you get fingerprints off of the wood?"

Reed looked at me incredulously, and I looked at the floor. "Oh, yeah, I guess not. Too dusty." He nodded, and I wondered if I had just gone down in his estimation.

On the other hand, why should I care if what he thinks I know about crime?

Why was I thinking about crime right then?

I suppose it was the writer in me. I was born curious.

"Are you going to lift the trap door?"

"Oh, yes," Reed said. "We'll have to. We can't get the body out if we don't."

"So when is that going to be?" I blurted out before I could stop myself.

"We have to make sure we don't disturb any evidence. So – it might be a while. You'll need to be patient." Reed started taking pictures of the trap door.

"I do have a business to run." I wasn't normally this impatient, but in spite of his politeness, something about this guy bothered me.

"And that will have to wait." He continued to take pictures.

"Was there something you wanted to ask me?" I said.

"Oh," Reed said. "I had wondered whether you had noticed anything suspicious."

"No," I said. "I haven't had a chance to get into the yard yet. I hadn't been out here in years." When Reed lifted his eyebrows, I added. "I just came back the other day. I haven't actually moved back into town yet."

"Ah."

"Can we go back into the office?" Ted said. "I'm getting cold."

"Oh. Yes." He looked as if he was waiting for us to

leave.

I was getting cold, too. I wasn't dressed warmly enough to spend much time in the yard. But I wanted – no, needed – to see what was going on. "If you move anything, I'd like to be outside here to see."

"For your curiosity?" Reed said. His voice had a little bit of an edge in it.

"No." I said sharply, although that was part of it. "Because I'm the President of this company, and I think I should know exactly what's going on in my yard." I took a step toward him and stared up at him.

He looked down at me. Seriously, he wasn't bad looking, but at that point, I was annoyed and only later did I realize that his eyes were the deepest blue I had ever seen. And the black hair, touched with silver, was nice, too.

He backed off without moving. "Yes. I suppose you do. I will let you know." I could see he was reluctant, but, after all, it was my right as owner. "As long as you don't get in the way."

"Of course," I said, coldly. I started walking back to the office, and Ted fell in beside me.

When we got into my office, Ted turned to me. "You made him uncomfortable out there." His voice was mild, but I felt like he was accusing me.

"Good," I said, collapsing in the chair. "I almost felt like I was doing his job for him. I mean, that deal with the shavings? How did they miss that?" I was still a bit peeved. "Makes me wonder what else they missed."

"Well," Ted said. "This is a small town. It's not we have a large criminal unit." He took the other chair and looked out the window.

I smiled, in spite of myself. "I suppose," I said, "that I've been trained to be detail oriented these past fifteen years."

"With numbers," Ted said mildly. "Not with police work."

"Granted. But I keep thinking about writing mystery fiction," I said.

"Really?" Ted said. "Marie loves cozies."

But I was digressing. I brought my attention back to Ted. "Did Joe have any enemies?"

Ted's eyebrows lowered, and he looked at the opposite wall. He snorted slightly. "I heard that he was in World War II, but came out of the army like – what you saw. I suppose you could say that the German Army was his enemy."

"PTSD?"

Ted cocked his head. "PTSD?"

"Post-Traumatic Stress Disorder," I elaborated. "Do they think that's what he had?"

Ted grinned. "No. They used to call it exhaustion. They would pull soldiers out of the front line, then send them back in when they felt better. It just persisted in Ted. I understand you never wanted to get around him when he had a nightmare." He brought his attention back to me. "I don't think he remembered the War a lot. I think he was so successful in blocking it out, that he ended up like this."

"Still. Who would have hated him now?"

"I can't imagine." Ted shook his head. "The only thing I can think of is that some stranger in town robbed him for money."

"He had to have been in his upper eighties," I mused. "And he looked like he couldn't beat a fly. It would have been much easier to push him down and go through his pockets. Why kill him?"

"He was obviously stronger than he looked."

"Possible. Still." I picked up a pen and started doodling on the scratch pad. "Why didn't they take the ring? Class rings have gold in them. The robber could have sold it." I doodled some more. "And why drag him to building number three to dump his body? How did the murderer even get in the building?"

"Oh, that's easy. He lifted up the door." He shrugged. "We lock the building, but that doesn't mean somebody strong couldn't go through one of the barn doors on the buildings."

I blinked. "The yard was surrounded by chain link."

"I didn't tell you before, but we found the chain link fence cut a couple of days ago. It was around the back gate." He saw my expression. "It's already been fixed."

"Did you tell Reed?"

"Yes."

"What about surveillance cameras?"

Ted wrinkled his forehead. "We don't have any. I thought you knew that."

"What is that one in the corner?"

"Um. That was your Dad's joke. He didn't see the necessity for surveillance cameras. Or monitoring. He thought the big safe was enough of a deterrent." The big safe looked like it might have come out of a bank. It was a walk in safe with a fireproof room. It might give a serious thief pause, or it might just tempt him to bang the hell out of it trying to get it open. Neither option was great, in my mind.

"You're kidding."

Ted shrugged. "Well, we haven't been broken into yet."

I closed my eyes. "You were lucky."

"You planning on bringing in one of those cameras?"

"I'll have to think about it." Which meant that I had better talk with Mom, first. Surveillance equipment, computers—I was starting to get into big ticket stuff, and I still had to scope out Mom's personal situation, first.

I got up. "I need to go out into the main office and watch." And worry.

<<<<>>>>

An hour later we were still waiting, although they

had finally processed Mark and Buford and let them go. I looked out the office window at building number three. The big green building was surrounded with yellow tape, and the police were taking pictures of evidence. There weren't too many detectives and I suspect they called some in from other places; Herculaneum wasn't that big, and they only had a murder once every twenty years, I think. I saw that Officer Reed was still there, looking around.

Which was why the big cities got the CSI departments. Here, they probably had one elderly guy in a lab coat that looked like Bob Newhart. If that.

We had been answering the phone, setting up orders for the next day, and telling customers why we couldn't deliver for the day. Some of our customers were understanding, others were hot under the collar. Being the new kid on the block, I stayed out of the arguments, only jumping in when I absolutely needed to. One notable contractor threatened to sue if we didn't get his delivery out right then; I offered to let him argue with the police. He got very quiet after that; I found out later that he had a record of public drunkenness and was once charged with attacking an officer. I vowed not to get into a physical argument with him.

The phone rang again. Ted answered and got a funny look on his face. "Just a second," he told the person on the phone, then handed it to me.

"Trouble?" I said.

"You might say that," he said, holding his hand over the mouthpiece. "It's your mother."

I noticed the time. "Oh, crap." I sprinted towards my office to get the phone there.

"Mom. I'm sorry, I didn't notice the time..."

"Aren't you going to have lunch?"

"I forgot." I didn't want to go on to tell her why I forgot.

She seemed almost unnaturally calm, for her. "Is there anything you want to tell me?"

57

"Mom. There's been a murder here."

"I know."

I blinked and looked at the base of the phone, like I could see her face in the keypad. "You know."

"This is a small town," she said. "I was at church, helping them fold newsletters, and Al Smithson's wife got a phone call. Al told her."

"You don't seem upset."

"Honey, I've lived around this town all of my life. Nothing surprises me anymore."

"Surprise is one thing. Upset is another."

"Okay," she said. "I'm a little upset. Do you know who was murdered yet?"

"Joe Newton." The phone was silent. "Mom?"

"Now that surprised me," she said slowly. "Why would anyone kill old Joe?"

"I don't know," I said. "I haven't lived here in years."

"And whose fault was that?" Her voice was slightly teasing, so I didn't rise to the bait. Her voice turned serious. "Can you leave?"

"I suppose so. They haven't said we can't leave, but they would prefer that we not deliver orders."

"I take that back. Let me pick something up for everybody."

"What do you have in mind?" I hoped it wasn't McDonald's. I have nothing against McDonald's; I just didn't think I could choke a burger down right now.

"I'll surprise you. I'll be there in a half an hour."

She was right, she did surprise me. She went to the store and picked up cold cuts, fancy veggies, fresh fruit, and cookies. Ted called Sam and Mathew in, and we sat around the office, watching the police. If this hadn't been so serious, it would have been riveting to watch. The guys sat around, making nasty comments.

"Aren't they ever going to pull poor old Joe out of

there?" Mom said.

"I suppose they need to be thorough, Marie," Ted said.

"Still," she fussed, "it just seems too disrespectful to leave him there under building number three."

A man walked in, and I felt like running screaming out into the street. How had he found me here? Well, I suppose I had told him once where my father worked, so he must have figured it out. "Vince. What are you doing here? Go away."

"But baby, I want to see you."

Subtle, my ex-fiancé.

The guys were frankly staring at him. Ted had gotten up and stood beside me. "May I help you?"

"I just want to talk to my fiancé here."

"Vince," I said, "you are not my fiancé. I do not want to see you anymore, and I've made that abundantly clear to you. What are you doing in Herculaneum?" Now, that was a stupid statement. I knew what he was doing here. But I suppose I had to ask it.

He looked pitiful. "You left your apartment. You didn't give me your address. That's not a way that you should treat a fiancé."

The rest of the men started getting up. "I believe," Ted said, "the lady told you to leave."

"Not until..."

"Vince," I said, "give up. Find another girlfriend. I told you this weeks ago."

"But you're my..." he whined.

"Vince," I said. "Do you see those men out there?"

For the first time, his attention focused on something else besides me. "Yeah. Are those police?"

"They are. So I would recommend that you leave."

"What are they there for?"

"None of your business." Although I suppose if he hung around, the story would be in the paper, such as it

59

was, on Saturday. Or the nightly news from Kalamazoo.

"If they think you did something, I'll protect you."
Vince started to look threatening.

My mouth dropped open. I had never considered that angle.

"Vince," I said, "how long have you been in town?"

"Long enough." He managed to look smug and threatening at the same time. All of the guys had stood up and moved to the counter.

"Well," I said, pointing to the police outside, "don't leave town. *They* might want to talk to you."

He looked at me, he looked at the police, and he looked at the guys who were moving around the counter. "You'll never be anything without me," he hissed, then abruptly ran out the door.

Ted stared after him. "Should I call the police the next time he's in here?"

I leaned on the counter, tired. "Probably wouldn't be a bad idea," I said. "He's never been violent, but he has been annoying."

"Do you have a restraining order on him?" Ted said.

"No, but I should have." I sighed. "When we started dating, I really liked him. Then he started making comments about my friends and my co-workers."

"You don't need to say any more," Mathew said. "I know some people like that." Cody nodded, too. Jimmy just looked at me, and Sam looked at the office. Mom stared me in the face, and I knew I would have to unload to her later. I knew she knew some of it, but she didn't know all of it.

Not having a job sucked. Not having a job and having a boyfriend like that was beyond sucky, it went into dangerous territory.

Gradually, the talk turned back to the murder, and — shame on me — I was seriously relieved. I truly didn't want to discuss my love life with a bunch of guys, even if they were friendly. I realized with a shock that they were my employees. "You know," I said, "they seem to be concentrating on barn number three. I think I need to get out there and push some buttons and see if we can do some work that doesn't involve barn three."

"I'll come with you," Ted said.

"No," I said. "I'm going to need to do this by myself eventually."

"I'm not sure..." Ted said quietly, then he motioned me back to my office. "I'm not sure that Reed will listen to you."

"Why not?"

"He's a bit of an old bachelor, if you know what I mean." Ted shook his head. "I mean, he's not against woman, but his first wife was a doozy. Cheated on him numerous times."

"A doozy, huh?" I smiled. My smile faded. "He'll just have to get over it if he wants to deal with me." I grabbed my coat and a walkie-talkie and strode purposely out of the office, wondering in my heart of hearts whether I was doing the right thing. My heart shrank back from confrontations, but my mind said that I needed to do this now, in front of the guys, or I would lose any chance of, well, commanding them later. Taking my father as my guide, I strode up to Officer Reed.

"Officer," I said, "we've been sitting in our office for three hours. I need to find out whether you'll release our yard soon so that we can start to make deliveries or whether I'll need to send everybody home."

Officer Reed stood up from the trap door, looking rather constipated. "What do you mean?"

"I need to know if your investigations are just in this one building, or whether you intend on keeping the whole yard captive while you play around in that hole."

His eyebrows rose. "We still haven't gotten the body out," he said.

"I know. What's the delay?" I peered down into the

hole. A couple pair of policemen's eyes looked back at me. "Rats?"

"We're *trying* to do a thorough investigation here." All of which implied that I was impeding that investigation.

Yeah, right.

I grabbed his flashlight and peered in the hole, myself. Unfortunately, this revealed the face and the filmed over eyes of old Joe and the dried blood on his shirt. I turned the flashlight the other direction. "Have you looked over there?" I shone the flashlight in the far corner of the barn. A bunch of trim had been messed up and had fallen over. Knowing my father, I knew that he would never stand for this.

Reed shrugged. "Why would we?"

"Because *we* keep our stock neat."

"How would *you* know? You just started here."

"I am my father's daughter. You think I wouldn't know how he would run a yard?"

I wasn't entirely sure how he ran the yard, but that wasn't the point. I would have to learn my own style, but, until then, I could use what my father had said at home. I wished I had actually worked here at one point, but I was adamant about not working at the lumberyard and hadn't regretted that decision — up until now.

Reed stared at me and pursed his lips. "You do realize that we can shut down the whole yard until I'm satisfied."

Officer Cole walked up. I wished I had thought to get his first name. "Detective?" he said. He glanced at me. "I believe we're through processing the rest of the yard. I did find some blood spatter in the saw room, but I think it was old."

I remember hearing about that one. Sam had sawed off the end of his finger to the first joint just a couple of years ago. Dad spouted off to me about how stupid that was, saying that I would have to watch Sam when I became the owner.

I had put it out of my mind. I had thought that Dad was going to live for a long, long time, and he was going to turn it over to one of employees to do the day-to-day running when he retired. Or so I figured.

"Talk to Sam," I said. "That may be from his finger. I doubt if they cleaned the saw room too thoroughly."

Officer Cole smiled. "Oh, yeah, I remember that now."

"I'll look at it," Reed said, "and I'll talk to Kline." He closed his eyes. "Have the boys gone over the rest of the yard?"

No female police? I shrugged. Ah, small town life.

"Yeah," said Reed. "Apart from the cut in the fence in the back, the yard looks clean."

"Then get Austin in here to take the body."

I looked puzzled.

"John Austin," Officer Cole explained. "Mark's cousin. He's the undertaker."

"No coroner?"

"And the coroner," Cole said.

"The coroner is a medical doctor and an undertaker?"

Cole shrugged. "Decided he had better luck with dead patients than live ones, I guess."

I smiled uncertainly. "So can we start delivering?" I called after Reed.

He turned and fixed those blue eyes on me and sighed. "Except for this barn and the saw room," he said.

I picked up the walkie-talkie. "Yard to Office."

Ted picked up the walkie-talkie. "Office," he said. I could see him smile.

"It's a go. The saw room and this barn are off limits."

"Got it. We can work around that."

"Tell Sam that Officer Reed will need to see his

hand to double-check that he actually did cut off his finger. They found blood in the saw room."

I could see the guys snicker. "They'll probably find more blood than Sam's in there. I think we've all cut ourselves in there."

I wrinkled my forehead. "Aren't the safety guards on?"

Ted could be seen looking at Sam. "They are now."

"Ah." I was glad they couldn't see me rolling my eyes. But I could see my mother, and she was giving them a piece of her mind. A couple of them slunk out of the office.

Reed was walking down to the saw room stiffly. I could almost see the broomstick up his... back. My eyes dropped from his back.

Actually, he did have a nice behind.

I jerked my eyes away from him. "Let me know when Austin comes," I told Officer Cole. "I'd like to pay my respects."

"Will do, ma'am."

I had never been a ma'am before. I liked the sound of that.

At least I wasn't a madam, said the rogue part of my brain.

I walked back to the office. Sam gave me a dirty look on the way out.

What was that for? I acted like I hadn't seen it and vowed to ask about it later.

CHAPTER 5

I arrived home, walked in, and collapsed on the chair, and closed my eyes. "What a day." I groaned.

Mom, who had left the yard in the middle of the afternoon after old Joe was brought out, came out of the kitchen. "I thought we would go out to supper tonight."

I pried my eyelids open and looked at her. "Mom. For God's sake, why tonight?"

"It's good PR. We need to show that we're strong and won't buckle, even under murder."

I wrinkled my nose. "Why would anybody think that?"

"Oh," she said. "You grew up here. You know it's a small town. Do I really have to tell you?"

"Yes," I said, sitting up.

"The rumor going around town is that you're running away from an abusive boyfriend and only took this job because it got you away from him. And Ted is actually the power behind the yard."

"What?" Well, part of that was true. Part of it was that I had lost my job and didn't have much of another choice. Part of it was because Daddy wanted me to take over the yard. And Ted is the head right now, until I get my feet under me again. And then Vince showed up.

There were a lot of reasons. But the road ran both ways from Detroit to here, as Vince obviously had demonstrated.

"What do I have to do to convince them otherwise?"

"Show yourself in public. Take care of your appearance."

"Mom," I said. "I was accused today of dressing too high for the yard."

"Designer jeans," she promptly said. "Good shirts,

but not too good."

I flopped back. "The last thing I want to do tonight is show myself off to Mrs. Grundy." Grundy was our term for old lady know-it-alls.

"I know," Mom said calmly. "That's why you have to." She picked my coat back up and tossed it at me. "Come on. You're not getting supper here."

We went to the Hop-In restaurant, one of our local family diners. I sat in a rickety chair, and I noticed three calendars on the walls. According to some wags, that meant that the food was great here. I didn't remember being here, until I saw the malted milk machines in the corner.

Then I remembered.

Amazing how food brings things back.

The diner smelled delicious. It smelled like all of those things I didn't want to eat anymore because I was eating healthy. It smelled of hamburgers and cheeseburgers and fries and open-faced hot beef sandwiches and fried fish in batter. I felt like I was gaining ten pounds through my pores just sitting here.

The diner, which had gone silent when we walked in, buzzed with talk and gossip. I suspect some of it was about me.

I did say that this was a small town, right?

But, then again, I could have gotten this kind of treatment in a big city.

I looked around, in the corners and at the counter. Yes, Mrs. Grundy and her friends were here. And their husbands. In fact, I think if a teenager walked in, the average age of the restaurant would go down twenty-five years. But what I was looking for was Vince. I half expected to see him in the corners. But I didn't — I don't suppose he could find this place, at least right away. It wasn't anywhere near a McDonald's or burger row. And, as I remember, his veins practically bled ketchup.

"Marie," said one Mrs. Grundy, coming up. I

66

smelled her strong perfume and tried to cough delicately, so she wouldn't realize that I was coughing because of her. She gave Mom a half hug. "How are you doing?"

Mom gave her a half smile. "Oh, as fine as can be expected." She turned to me. "Carrie, I don't know if you remember Ellen Carter?"

I turned to her and extended my hand. "Yes, I believe so. From church?"

"Yes." She sat down on the other chair with a sigh. Drinking my cola, I studied her. She had white hair. Her glasses perched on the end of her nose, and I wondered if she actually needed them, or whether they were for the effect. She had a blue sweatshirt with cardinals stitched down the front. Her polyester slacks were gray. Her face had a perpetual frown on it, until she smiled, then her whole face lit up. She talked with a slight southern accent, so I gather she wasn't originally from Michigan.

I realized that it was my turn to speak. "Excuse me?"

"I said," Ellen said, "are you going to move in with your mother?"

"I guess so," I said. I looked at my mother. We hadn't really discussed it. She nodded. "I am, for a while. But I have a ton of stuff to get rid of in Detroit." I thought about it. I had never actually moved a lot of my old stuff out of the house, and the furniture I had was old and worn. "I lived in an apartment over there."

"I'm surprised that you never settled down." Meaning — why wasn't I married?

"I never found the right man. I thought I had, a couple of times, but they turned out to be frogs, not princes." Especially Vince. "And all of the good guys were married." And, let's face it, while I enjoyed the big city, I never did actually feel at home over there.

"When are you planning to move here?"

"As soon as possible. After the first year there, I

never renewed my lease on the apartment. I went month by month."

"I understand you lost your job over there?" Ellen looked sharply at me.

"The company I worked for went under." Actually, the CPA I worked for had gotten sick and retired, but that was none of her business. "I hadn't found a new job yet," I sighed.

Her face looked sympathetically at me, but I had a feeling she wondered why I couldn't find another job. In this economy? Really? I suspected that my age had a little to do with it. Even though I was only a little older than forty, I had the feeling that all of my interviewers were looking for twenty-year-olds that they could pay less and not pay for insurance. The job market sucked these days.

However, I never wanted to take my Dad's job. Especially like this.

"I know," she said. "My grandson is looking for a job, and it's hard out there."

I hoped she wasn't looking for me to hire him. I wasn't sure how the company worked, much less whether we need new employees.

"He lives in the Chicago area."

Phew. "It's tough all over," I said.

"So," she said. "It's a shame about old Joe, huh? Do they know what happened to him yet?"

"If they have," I said, pulling another drink on my cola, "they haven't told me." I thought about the crime scene. "Do you know why Joe wore a class ring backwards on his finger?"

Ellen looked at the opposite wall. "You knew that he was in World War II."

I nodded.

"And when he came back, he was never the same."

"Post-Traumatic Stress Disorder." I nodded.

"But, back then, they didn't call it that. We called it

68

battle fatigue, or worse, we called them yellow cowards."
She shook her head. "At least, that's what Patton called it.
Some people couldn't handle the stress of war."

"But what does that..."

"Before the war, he was married to a wonderful
woman. She was the light of his life." She smiled. "She
used to be a friend of mine."

"After the war?"

"She couldn't stand what he had become. You see,
she thought he was yellow, too. She divorced him and left
town." Ellen sighed. "That was the last nail in his coffin."

"Where did she go?"

"She died a couple of years ago," Ellen said.

"Were there any children?"

Ellen shrugged. "One. Don't know what happened
to her."

"Ah."

"So he wore his class ring backward because he was
married?"

"And it looked like a wedding ring. At least in his
mind."

How sad. Seventy years of longing for a woman
who abandoned him because she thought he was a coward.
No wonder he retreated into a fantasy life.

"What about other family?" I said.

"His parents took care of him as long as they were
able. His brother was killed in Korea." Ellen mused. "I had
heard that the Newtons had money, but I don't know where
it went. I think most of it still goes for his care."

"Such as it was," I muttered.

Mom nodded. "Certainly wasn't used on his clothing."

Our food came at that point. I had gotten the open-
faced roast beef sandwich, and I could feel my thighs ex-
panding just looking at it. Mom, more sensible, had a
chicken breast salad.

Ellen got up to leave. "Well, it was nice to talk to you."

"Nice to re-meet you!" I said, standing up.

Ellen toddled away and went back to her table. "See?" Mom said quietly. "The rumors will go around, but at least they'll go our way now."

I grinned slightly. "I never realized that you were so cynical, Mom."

"Don't get me going, dear," she smiled. "I just know how to play the game."

"So who do you think killed Joe?"

"I think," she said reflectively, taking a small bite of salad, "that we don't know enough about the circumstances. Why would anybody dump him in building number three? In fact, how did they get in there without anybody noticing? Or if they went in after hours, why bother to cut the fence to dump him in there?"

All good questions. "Maybe we'll need to ask around."

She nodded. "I wouldn't expect much out of the police."

"I got that impression," I said, digging into the mashed potatoes. "Although Stetson Reed is good looking." I blushed. "Did I say that out loud?"

"You did, and he is," Mom said. "Even if he isn't the most observant guy in the world."

"Did I say that?"

"I talked to Ted."

"Ah."

"I've known him since he was a kid," Mom said. "He's not dumb."

"How come I don't remember him?"

"I think he's about five years younger than you are."

Which would be why I wouldn't remember him. I never spent a substantial amount of time in town after I went to college. So if I were seventeen, I never would have noticed a twelve-year-old kid.

As if to shame me, my roast beef sandwich came with a salad, to appease my sense of eating healthy. I took a nibble of salad. "I should talk to his caregivers." I said, musing out loud.

"Joe's or Stetson's?" Mom said, with a grin.

I realized that I had made one of those non-sequitur jumps in my mind without saying anything out loud. But Mom knew me and figured that I was back on Joe's death.

"Joe's," I said, taking another piece of salad. "Something about his life story bothers me."

"That he was driven mad by war? Or that he ended up dead in the lumber yard?"

I shook my head. "I can't verbalize it yet."

"I would wait," Mom said. "You can talk to his caregivers at his funeral."

"Do you know them?"

She shook her head.

"Does anybody know them?"

"They don't run in the same circuit that we're in," Mom said. "I understand that they're rather reclusive. Joe wasn't their only charge, either."

"Hmmm. I still think I want to talk to them."

Mom took a delicate bite of her salad. "I understand that one of your classmates is under their care."

I blinked at her. "One of mine? Really?"

"Ashley Weedman."

"Oh." I remembered Ashley. I was her "lab part-ner," so to speak, in Middle School, which meant I did the experiments and tried to explain the results to her. I believe she had the mental level of a first grader — enough to func-tion, but not enough to take care of herself competently. Maybe I could talk with her. "I'm surprised that they have men and women together in the same home."

"It was a new home for Joe," Mom said. "Besides,

he was together enough that he wouldn't make a move on a young girl. I've heard he hadn't touched anybody since his wife had left."

"Well, that's something," was the only thing I could think to say. I dug into my roast beef thoughtfully.

The next day, I was at the Daytimers Foster Home, wondering why in the world I was there. I knocked on the door, and a pleasant looking, middle aged lady answered. She smiled at me. "Yes?"

"I wanted to talk to the owners of this foster care about Joe?"

"Okay." She closed the door, and I could see her wander away into the living room and sat down. One of the residents.

I knocked on the door again. The lady got up again and answered the door. "Yes," she said, pleasantly.

I stuck my foot into the jamb. "Can I talk to the owners?"

"Yes." She started to close the door. When the door wouldn't close, she became agitated.

Another woman hurried up, her gray hair helter-skelter. She looked upset. "What's going on here?"

"Are you the owner?"

"Yes, but things are very upset here. I can't buy anything."

I smiled reassuringly. "I'm not selling anything. I'm the President of Herculaneum Lumber. We discovered..." I couldn't go on.

The lady stared at me. "Oh," she said, and I was beginning to wonder whether she was another resident. "Oh, I'm sorry. I'm Mary Devin." She held out her hand. "I thought the president was a man."

I felt a wave of sorrow and firmly pressed beyond it. "It was. My father. He passed away a couple of weeks ago."

Her face turned kind. "I'm sorry."

"Thank you." I looked beyond her. "May I come in?"

"Oh. Of course." She ushered me into the living room. The house was fairly large and had multiple bedrooms. The first woman I had met sat staring at the TV. "This is Grace." Grace smiled at me, then looked back at the TV.

Another man walked in with a walker. "This is Harry." The elderly black man looked up at me and waved. "She's here to talk to me about Joe," she said.

"Joe was a good man," Harry said. "A little nuts, maybe..."

Mary smiled at him. "Harry's here because of a walking problem."

Right. Which meant that he had his marbles.

Another woman walked in. I glanced at her, then looked at her again. "Ashley?"

She looked at me. It was Ashley.

"Do you remember me?"

"You were in Mrs. Al-Turk's class."

I smiled. "I was your classmate, but I wasn't in Mrs. Al-Turk's class."

Mary gave me a questioning look. "Mrs. Al-Turk was the special education teacher."

"Ah."

Mary headed toward the kitchen. "Can I get you a drink?"

"No, thank you," I said. "I just came — I feel kind of responsible for Joe. I just wanted to find out more about him."

"I can't say that I know his history too much," Mary said. "I listened to what he said, but half of what he said didn't make any sense."

"Like..."

"'Thar's gold in them thar hills.'" Mary laughed, but

a small tear came down her face. "'Wanna buy a newspaper, squire?' A couple of other things."

"Do you think they made sense to him?"

"Oh," she said. "I suppose."

"How old was he?"

"Eighty-five."

"I heard that he had a family. Did they ever visit?"

Mary shook her head. "If he did, they never visited here. We were the only family I know of."

"I miss Joe," Ashley said. "He helped me cut out paper dolls."

"Yes, Ashley," Mary said. "He did. We'll have to do an activity to remember Joe." She turned to me. "Ashley likes to do activities."

Ashley nodded. "Joe said that his family had a farm. With chickens and pigs and cows."

"I heard," Mary said, "that Joe's family was quite influential around here in the twenties, then the collapse came and the family lost everything during the depression."

Ashley nodded. "He said he had gold!"

I shrugged. "Maybe." I sighed. "I'm just figuring out why anyone would want to mur..." I looked at Ashely. "Hurt an eighty-year-old man who wasn't harming anybody."

Mary frowned. "You'd be surprised. You should see what people do when I take the residents here out for a movie." She shook her head. "People can be so cruel."

"They can," I said. "They can."

I yawned as I got home. These nine-hour days were killing me — poor choice of words. Mom had made some home-made macaroni and cheese, and I reflected that if I wanted to keep any semblance of my current figure, I was going to have to lay off the casseroles. Maybe I would have to eat supper out.

Then I looked at my Mom. This wasn't exactly her

fare, either. She was overcompensating.

"Mom," I said, "delicious as this was, I think we're going to have to lay off the carbs."

"I know," she sighed. "I was just thinking about your Daddy and this just sounded good."

"Comfort food." I took another forkful of Mac and Cheese. It did taste good going down. "But if we have too much comfort food, we're going to kill ourselves."

She stared into the distance. I was afraid she would think that that wasn't a bad idea.

"Mom?"

"You're right, of course," she said. She took a sip of tea. "You know, I always said that I could live without your father. I could live by myself, if I wanted to."

I nodded. "I know you can."

"But even though I know your Father's in heaven, and I know that I'll see him someday, I..." She couldn't finish the sentence. She shook her head angrily. "I refuse to feel sorry for myself."

"Grief is not necessarily feeling sorry for oneself," I said, trying to distance our emotions verbally. "It's natural to grieve for loved ones. Even if we're Christians."

Mom smiled. "You read that out of a book."

"You don't think I'm wise beyond my years?" I grinned.

"I think you are," she said, "But I read that book, too."

I grinned. "Made you smile, though, didn't I?"

"Oh, yes." She shook her head again. "I think you need to go to church this week."

"I had planned to sort..." I started. "Oh. Another one of those being seen in public?"

"Can't hurt." She sighed. "And we might find out something more."

I took a long drink of water, then pursed my lips. "I was told not to interfere in police business."

"Pshaw," she said. "Isn't that an interesting word?"

"Never heard it spoken out loud," I grinned. "Pshaw? Really?"

"I like the word. I saw it in a crossword."

"Really?" I shook my head. "I'm getting distracted. You were saying Pshaw?"

"Oh, yeah. I think we need to do our own little investigation here. Stetson Reed hasn't been to church in years, and it's amazing what the church ladies know."

"A little bit of coffee hour investigations?"

"Can't hurt."

I told her what I had found out at the foster care.

"It seems that he doesn't have any living relatives," Mom said. "But it could be that his estranged daughter is still choosing to be estranged."

"Is there any way we can find them?"

"Apart from going through every marriage record in the U.S. and seeing who Mrs. Newton's daughter married? I doubt it."

"Humph. Still, someone has to be around, don't they?"

Mom smiled at me sadly. "Some people don't have relatives, you know that."

I sat silent. Mom's parents had died young, she was an only child, and she had no cousins. I suppose that she had second or third cousins, but that was essentially no relation, wasn't it?

I didn't have any cousins, either. Nor aunts or uncles. We were much the same.

I felt even more sympathetic to old Joe.

"Joe didn't go to church, did he?"

"No, but some of the older ladies might know about his family. Of course, we'll have to be subtle about this."

I snickered. "With those ladies?"

We walked into church along the side entrance. I

hadn't been here in years. And I certainly didn't remember the hallways being that bright. I looked around. Brightly colored bulletin boards covered the halls. A hanging quilt with three crosses sewn in covered the end of the hallway. And the smells. I turned to my Mom. "Is that sugar cookies?"

She laughed at me. "It's the Coles' turn to do the hospitality table. They always bring fresh baked sugar cookies." She sniffed. "And some chocolate chip cookies, if my nose serves right."

I hadn't been to church in a while; apparently, I was missing something. "If this happens every week, then I'll have to come to church more often."

Mom rolled her eyes. "My dear, you don't have the right attitude."

"Yeah?"

"You're not supposed to come to church for cookies and coffee, you're supposed to come for the message and the fellowship," she said.

"But cookies don't hurt," I smiled. I leaned over toward her. "Besides, aren't we here in church to find out about Joe?" I said lowly.

"I'd like to think," she said, looking around, "that you'd come to church just because I wanted you to. Or, more important, because you wanted to."

"Mo-om. Coming because you wanted me to? I'm not twelve."

"I know, honey, I was kidding."

Yeah, sure you were. I smiled. To my Mom, I think I'll always be her gap-toothed baby girl. And that's all right.

I stood in the middle of the hall. I wasn't kidding when I said I hadn't been to church in a while. I believed; I just didn't see the necessity of organized religion. But people were greeting each other like family, there were cookies and coffee, I could hear the choir tuning up in a closed room, small children were chasing each other down the hall, and people were being greeted warmly as they entered the church. I sighed. Perhaps this is what people needed. A chance to feel like family. I was feeling sorry about old Joe not having a family, but he had people who loved him in that Foster Care facility. I was feeling sorry because Mom and I didn't have family, but we could have a family right here.

"Well," I muttered, "now I'm having a Hallmark moment." But it was true.

I shook myself. I was here for a purpose. I needed to ask about old Joe.

A little lady bustled up. "You must be Carrie Burton," she said, without preamble. "You probably don't remember me. I'm Liz Grant. You were one of my little Girl Scouts."

I blinked and smiled. "You're right. I don't remember." I was a Girl Scout—when? I think I flew up from the Brownies and that was it; I had quit. "How are you, Mrs. Grant?"

"I'm doing well," she said. "Just feeling a bit old." I looked at her, she was, maybe, seventy.

"I'm sorry I don't remember."

"Oh, that's not it, I always feel that way when I see one of my old scouts." She smiled to take the bite out of her words, then her smile turned sympathetic. "I was so sorry to hear about your father. It was so sudden. He was in church that Sunday, and he so looked like he was enjoying himself." *In church?* She must have seen my expression. "We had a kid's program."

"Oh. Yeah. He liked to talk to children. It's a shame my parents couldn't give me any brothers and sisters. He would have been a great father to a large family.

"Heart?"

I nodded. "We had no warning that his heart was bad." I felt a wave of sadness, and I felt like crying.

78

Mrs. Grant gave me a quick hug. "I know. I lost my husband last year. Stroke." Her eyes looked at the end of the hall, but I have a feeling she was seeing farther than that. "I know he's with the Lord, but sometimes that's hard to believe at three in the morning."

Might as well take the opportunity. "Did you hear about the man we found at the lumberyard?"

"Yes!" she said. "Old Joe Newton. What a shame. Have the police figured out what he was doing in that building?"

Under it, actually. "No. But I was curious about him. I understood he didn't have any family."

She gave a short sniff. "Oh, he had family, all right. He had his parents, until they both died. But he was married, and he had a small daughter."

"So I understand. Where did they go?"

She shrugged. "I understood his ex-wife and his daughter moved out West someplace. I read in the Bulletin that his wife had remarried and passed away a couple of years ago. It had his daughter's name — she married somebody named Simms, and apparently, she had a daughter, too. Or was it a son?" She took a moment and waved at somebody going by. "But that's all I know."

Which was more than I had known. "Hum."

"Did you know his parents had a room named after them?"

"No."

She led me to a classroom, then pointed at the plaque along the side of the door. "They contributed quite a bit of money for building improvements. When we built this new part, we dipped into the money they had left. It seemed only fair that we name part of the building after them."

"So they had quite a bit of money at one point."

"Yeah. I'm not quite sure where it all went. I mean, they left enough for Joe to be comfortable for the rest of his life..." which explained why he was in a foster home, those places weren't cheap. "... but I always had the impressions from my parents that there should be more." She snorted. "My father always said that old Joe's father was a rum-runner, and that's where he got his fortune."

I looked around. "So, technically, this building is built on illegal funds."

"It never was proved, though." She smiled. "So even if the money was made from rum, at least the Lord has turned it to good use."

That was one way of looking at it, I guess. "The building is nice and homey," I agreed.

"We try. We need to attract the younger people."

Oh, yes. I had been to some of the super churches over by Detroit. I wasn't impressed. I smiled.

"So. What do you do?"

"I'm sure you heard that I've taken over at the lumber yard."

"Do you have any lumber background?"

I laughed. "Very little. But my father thought I could learn. I was laid off from my job when the company went under, so I came back here."

"Well, good luck." She waved at somebody else. "So what do you do for fun?"

"I keep thinking about writing."

"Have you had anything published?"

Not if I haven't written much of anything. "No. But that's the goal someday."

She nodded sagely. "What kind of writing?"

"Mysteries, maybe. I've thought a little of Science Fiction and Fantasy."

She looked kind of blank, then brightened. "Like Star Trek?"

I closed my eyes. I had a feeling I knew what her next comment was going to be. "Yeah, kind of like Star Trek."

80

"Yeah, I've seen that Han Solo stuff. That was a good movie."

What could I say? I nodded. I didn't feel I could correct the lady in church. Besides, it wasn't important.

Mom came up. "It's about time to go into the sanctuary," she said. "Can I steal my daughter away?"

"Of course, Marie. Well, Carrie, it was nice to talk to you! I'll see you in church!" She smiled at her own wit.

I grinned uncertainly. "It was nice to talk to you, too."

"Learn anything?" Mom said softly, as we smiled at the greeter and took our bulletin.

"I learned that the Newtons were rumored to be rum runners," I said, as we slipped in a pew.

"I knew that they had money," Mom said. "But I hadn't heard that."

"Like I said. Rumor." I flipped through the bulletin. Under the prayer concerns was "'Friends and Family of Joe Newton on his death.'"

"I saw that," Mom said.

"I suppose I should go to the funeral." I laid the bulletin beside me.

"Yes," Mom sighed. "I should, too." She looked puzzled. "I wonder if he's going to have a funeral?"

"What do you mean?"

"Who's going to pay for it?"

"Hmmm..."

Just then, the organ stopped playing and the minister stood up. I sat up straight. If I was going to be in church, I suppose I shouldn't fall asleep in the first minute.

Actually, I was quite surprised. The minister I did remember—Reverend McLaren—was long gone and passed away. I remembered playing in these pews, because the Minister was far too boring to listen to. But this lady had the gift of connecting to the people without putting them to sleep — well, most of them, anyway. The little old

81

ladies and men still nodded off, but I suspect they would nod off at a no-holds-barred wrestling match.

Or maybe I had changed?

As soon as the final blessing was made, most of the church streamed back toward the Narthex. I followed the crowd, but this time, I stuck with Mom. I looked around. The hall was filled with half-remembered people, and I temporarily felt a little shy. These people, like Mrs. Grant, knew me when I was little—well, maybe not the younger ones, but most of them over sixty, I thought. One by one, they came up to give Mom a hug and be introduced to me. I hoped I would remember names later... but I doubted it.

The one couple who stood out were the Logans. They toddled up, and I understood why they had his and hers canes. The man looked up at me in a friendly fashion. He had the bushiest eyebrows I had ever seen. The woman had long hair, back in a loose bun. "So—you're Carrie."

What do you say to a comment like that? "Yes. Yes, I am." I smiled at him. They both smiled back.

Mom stepped in, like she did so well. "Carrie," she said smoothly. "You remember John and Elinor Logan?" Her voice gave me the out.

"Actually," I said, "I'm not sure. I think I remember you."

"They were the owners of the hardware store in town."

I looked at him, trying to imagine another couple of inches. "Oh, yes."

"They said that they remember the Newtons."

"Joe was one of my best friends," John said.

I held out my hands. "I'm sorry for your loss," I said. "I didn't get to know him that well."

He took my hands. "Oh, my dear, I lost him a long time ago. He never was right after the war." His voice was still sad.

"His parents were still alive then?" I didn't want to

interrogate this old man, but I felt I did need to find out more about old Joe.

"Oh, yes. I have to admit, they stepped right up. Until they passed away, he wanted for nothing." He sighed. "But when they passed away, we found that they didn't have as much left in their investments as we would have thought."

"You sound like you knew."

"Oh, yes. I was executor. The will didn't make a whole lot of sense—or, actually, it made sense, but it was incomplete. It was missing pages." He shook his head. "It seemed to refer to another investment, but we were never able to locate it."

"He didn't seem to miss it."

"No. But he might have been more comfortable."

Elinor placed a hand on his and smiled. "It's also too bad we weren't able to locate his daughter."

"Or his grandchild," I said.

"It's like they dropped off of the face of the earth."

"They didn't want to be associated with him?" I said.

"No. Shell shock, battle fatigue — whatever you call it these days — was seen as an act of cowardice."

"So I've been told," I said. "But it's truly just a mental disorder that could have been eased by counseling."

"Something that wasn't well known," Mr. Logan said, "was that he had a concussion in battle. He also had a Purple Heart. I have it at home. I was afraid to let him have it in the facility."

"So you were his guardian?"

"Technically," Mrs. Logan said. "Mostly we just made sure he had a place to stay."

"Ah." I waited a beat. "Do you have any idea why he was in our barn?"

"No," Mr. Logan said.

"I think I do," Mrs. Logan said.

"Yeah?"

"Wasn't his grandparent's house right around there?"

Mr. Logan raised his bushy eyebrows. "Oh, yes, it was, wasn't it?" He thought for another moment. "I believe that was one of their barns."

"I didn't realize it was that old." I thought a moment. "That would explain a couple of things."

Mrs. Logan tugged on his arm. "We need to get going."

I shook his hand again. "It was nice to see you both again. Thanks for the information."

"If you hear anything, let me know."

"I will. Thanks."

I turned toward Mom, who had wandered off. She was talking with Mrs. Grant. I approached them.

"Well," Mom said. "Did you enjoy the conversation?" She stared intently at me.

"Very — enlightening," I said. "Did you know that our barn number three was Joe Newton's grandparent's barn?"

"Say that five times real fast," Mom said. Mrs. Grant gave us an odd look. "Old family joke," Mom explained.

Mrs. Grant smiled uncertainly. "Are you doing anything for lunch?"

"No, not really," Mom said. "What are you thinking?"

"How about Dad's place?"

I opened my eyes wide. How old was Mrs. Grant's dad?

CHAPTER 6

Turns out that "Dad's Place" was another Mom-and-Pop place. This diner had a different sort of ambiance, almost sort of a Fifties retro look, with replicas of vinyl records and a jukebox in the corner. There was even a velvet Elvis. The place smelled of bacon and pancakes and eggs and coffee. It didn't look like much, but it smelled delicious.

I looked over the menu. "What's fried mush?" I asked.

"You've never had fried mush?" Mom said. "I haven't raised you right."

"It's fried cornmeal," Mrs. Grant said, "and I'm having some. I can give you a bite, if you want. I usually put just butter on it. "

I looked over the menu. "I guess I'll just have the chicken salad," I sighed, thinking of my figure. "I've been eating too much lately."

Gradually, I became aware of someone staring at us. I glanced over to one side, then the other, but I couldn't see anybody obvious. I had just about decided that my spidey sense was defective when Mom leaned over at me.

"We're being watched."

"I know," I whispered back. "But who?" I tried to look around again circumspectly.

"The man in the back corner."

"Do you know him?"

"No. You?"

I looked again, then remembered the first customer I had met. "Richard Nathan. He said that we carried crap."

"Carrie."

"I was quoting." I looked at Mrs. Grant. She was still staring at the menu.

"Any idea why he would be staring at us?"

"Apart from him being a nasty guy?"

"Apart from that."

"No."

He got up from the corner and walked toward our table. I cursed to myself. "Hello, Mr. Nathan!" I said, brightly. I looked at him. His hair was just as dirty as I remembered.

"Miss Burton, Mrs. Burton."

Mrs. Grant extended her hand. "I'm Liz Grant."

"Good to meet you, ma'am."

Ma'am? He had manners?

"I wanted to talk to you out of the store. May I sit down for a second?"

"Of course," I said, glancing at Mom.

He glanced at Mrs. Grant. "It just seems like the quality of lumber is going down at your company."

"I'm sure," I said, "that they buy as good a product as they possibly can."

"The number four boards used to be better."

"My husband said," Mom said, stressing the husband word, "that you are right. The quality of lumber is going down. It's because there's not as much old growth trees as there used to be."

I looked at Mom. I had never known she knew much about the yard.

"He tried to buy as good a product as he could with limitations of the market."

Go, Mom!

"Or so he said," Mom said, backing off.

"I'll look into seeing what we can do," I said. "But, in the meantime, maybe we can look through the boards a little better for you." And Ted will kill me when he finds out.

"That's all I want," he said. "A fair deal." He smiled. I hoped he wouldn't lean over and get his greasy hair over our water.

"Thank you for letting me know," I said.

He got up. "I'll continue to let you know." He wandered over to the checkout.

"I can't see," Mrs. Grant said, "how you can put up with such an unpleasant man. Why, I think he owns half the rental houses in town." She hesitated. "You know, he even rents that foster care that Joe was at."

My head snapped up. "Yeah?"

"Oh, yeah," Mrs. Grant said, perusing her menu again.

"That's why he buys cheap." Mom looked at her own menu, then at me. "Why buy good stuff for renters who are going to wreck the stuff anyway?"

I thought of my own philosophy. I truly believed that there are very, very few evil people. After all, no one thinks of themselves as evil. Richard Nathan was trying to get the best he could for as little as he could so that he wouldn't be out of money if someone wrecked his houses. Why chase good money after bad? I didn't have to like Richard to understand that.

So did the person who killed Joe think he was doing something good?

That made me wonder about Joe. I know he was in World War II, but a lot of men came back from the war with their sanity intact. What had happened with Joe to cause him to lose his sense? Was it the concussion? A concussion could do strange things.

"You know," I said. "I should have asked Mr. Logan whether Joe had written any letters back from the war."

Mrs. Grant and Mom stared at me. "Excuse me?" Mrs. Grant said.

I realized that I had taken a leap ahead and had left the world behind again. "Sorry," I muttered. "Just speculating out loud."

The waitress came up. I noticed that she looked upset. "Are you all right?" Mom said.

"I just learned that one of my customers had died."

"Joe?" I speculated.

"Yeah."

"You hadn't heard before this?"

"I was out of town," she said.

"Sara," Mom said, "he was elderly. Surely you knew this was going to happen someday."

"I know," Sara said. "But he was such a *nice* old man."

And here was a perfect example of the dichotomy of people. One person regarded old Joe as crazy. The next regarded him as a nice elderly old man. One thought he was amusing, the next thought that he was a pitiful case. No doubt the Germans saw him as a formidable enemy, until something happened. He was probably a loving father and a doting son. Different things to different people.

And somebody saw him as a threat. An eighty-year-old man who seemed like he barely knew the time of day was a threat.

"I'm sorry," the waitress said. "What can I get you?"

Justice for an old man?

"I'll have the chicken salad," I said.

I couldn't give him justice on an empty stomach, could I?

CHAPTER 7

I sipped my coffee at 6:45 A.M. on Monday morning, looking out at the showroom floor. The one thing I wasn't used to was the hours. I had been working thirty-five to forty hours a week at my old job, maybe more in tax season, but this fifty-hour week was going to kill me, I knew it. I knew, as President and owner's daughter, I could probably have more time off, even set my own hours, but that just didn't seem fair.

But it just didn't seem natural yet to start work before the sun was up.

I got up from behind my desk and walked around. I needed to price invoices, but it was so boring. Most of it was no-brainers: look up the price in a book and put it down on an invoice. Costing the invoice — which means writing down the cost that we bought the item for — was much the same. For the special-order items, I was getting help from Ted.

This was why we needed to think about getting computers. Much more accurate.

I was also learning to build houses — not swinging a hammer, but from books. I figured that the practical stuff would come later, perhaps the middle of June, not in the cold weather of November. Like everything, there was a house building book for dummies, and, apart from watching some television shows, I was completely ignorant. And, reading through the books, I suspected that I wouldn't be estimating any plans soon, but that could come later, too.

I passed by the front showroom window and stopped. There on the opposite side of the street was Vince. Vince the creepy ex-fiancé. I walked fast across the showroom and started looking at the trim, getting out of sight of the window.

Jimmy stared at me, then got up and joined me.

89

"Carrie," he said, "are you all right?"

"No. Vince was out there."

I had told all of the guys about Vince, and he looked alarmed. "Do we need to call the police?"

"As long as Vince stays across the street and doesn't enter, no, I'm fine."

Jimmy peeked around the show room window and looked at the street. "He's not there."

I looked. He was gone.

Do I have a picture of Vince at home? No. But I think I still had one at my apartment. I chewed my lip.

"Listen, guys," I said. "Vince is still here. He's followed me over here and it doesn't look like he's going to leave. I'll get you a picture, but I would appreciate it if you didn't let him in."

"What did he do?" Cody said.

I sighed. "He was one of those men who didn't want me to talk to my friends, much less to other guys. He wanted me to himself all of the time."

"But," Cody said, "you weren't dating other guys?"

"No. There's just not a whole lot of single guys out there my age."

I could see Cody and Jimmy look at each other. "I know a few guys..." Cody said, with a grin.

"Contractors?" I pretended to shiver. "No, thank you."

"I'll tell Stubby and Sparky," Jimmy said.

"Stubby and Sparky?"

"Sam and Matt." Just then, Mathew came in, carrying a clip board. "Hey, Sparky."

"Yeah." Mathew placed his delivery invoice in the drawer, then turned to look at us.

"We got a guy that we don't want to let in the yard. His name is..." Jimmy turned to me.

"Vince. Vince Wadler. He's six-foot tall, blond, scraggly beard, overweight."

Mathew snorted.

"What?"

"That's half of our customers."

He was right. "I'll bring in a picture. Anyway, there's no reason for him to be in this place. He lives over in Detroit."

"Then why would he be here?" Cody said.

I blinked. Seriously, why would he be here before eight on a Monday morning? He had a job, didn't he? "I just saw that person for a second. Maybe it wasn't him. Still, if you see him..."

"We'll throw him out."

"And let me know. I'll see if I can charge him with stalking." I walked back to my office. Did I imagine him? I looked at the office window.

He was at the end of the block. He was staring at the building.

Oh, God.

I decided to go out after him — perhaps not the smartest thing to do, but I had to make sure it was him. I grabbed my coat and went out the front door. I saw the guys look startled, but I was on a mission. "Vince!"

"Well, look who's deigning to talk to me," Vince drawled, his voice hard. His eyes looked me up and down. "Babe, why don't you answer my phone calls? You're my fiancé."

"I was with my mother, and I am not your fiancé. Why don't you go back to Detroit?"

"And leave you with those... men?" He actually looked concerned, which was a bit alarming.

"I'm moving back here. And those men happen to be my employees."

Vince snickered. "You must be kidding. Your daddy left the company to you?"

"No, Vince, Dad did not leave the company to me."

91

I turned on my heels. Why did I think I was going to convince him to leave me alone? "He left the company to my mother."

"A lumberyard? Women can't run lumberyards," he said with a sneer, and I stared at him. I had never seen anybody sneer before since the talkies came to town. "It's not in their genetics."

"I am not talking about this with you."

Vince grabbed my arm.

"Let me go!"

"Not until I talk sense into you."

Did he actually think he was doing me a favor? "Let me go. Now."

"We need to talk."

"What do you think we've been doing?"

Suddenly, his arm was jerked back. "I believe the lady told you to let her go."

"Who are..." I looked back. His eyes were fixated on the gun in his face.

"That," I said, "would be the police. I suggest you do what he says."

"Where's your badge?"

"Are you sure," Detective Reed said, "that you want me to let go of my gun to get my badge? It might slip."

"The badge?"

"The gun. And it's got a sensitive trigger."

Vince actually gulped. I saw his Adam's apple go up and down.

"So I suggest you leave the lady alone."

He held up his hands, backed off, and walked down the street. But he turned to look at me as he walked to his car, and I knew he would be back.

"Thank you, Detective Reed," I said, as soon as the car was out of sight.

He pretended like he was blowing the barrel of the gun. "Good thing he didn't realize that the gun wasn't loaded."

I blinked. "Why not? You're a police detective. Your gun should be loaded."

Even in the early morning light, I could tell that he blushed. "I unload it at night. I forgot today."

I suppressed a snort. "So, Detective, what brings you this direction today?"

"I wanted to ask you a couple of questions."

"Oh." We walked in silence back to the office. He held the door open for me, and the guys stared at us and we walked in. "What did you need to ask?" I motioned for Ted to join us.

"I wanted to see if I could look at your employee records."

I stiffened. "Why would anyone *here* kill a helpless old man?"

He pursed his lips. "It's so I can eliminate any of your employees. But the question I keep coming back to is — why here? Why under your barn?"

I had wondered that myself. But I had an obligation. "I've been through the records. I can't imagine what would be in there that would help you."

He frowned. "I'd like to see that for myself."

I stopped in the aisle. "What if I don't want to let you?"

He exhaled angrily. "I could get a subpoena."

"And maybe I'll make you get one!" I said, angrily. I know, I know, he rescued me from Vince, but this man pushed all of my wrong buttons.

Ted came up to us. "Carrie, it'll do no harm to let the Detective look at the records, will it?"

I turned angrily towards Ted. Suddenly, my anger faded. "No, you're right. As long as that's all you look at."

"That was all I was planning to look at," he retorted. "But..." He stopped talking after a look from Ted. "Yes, that was all I wanted to look at."

"Thank you for scaring Vince," I said, sincerely.

He acted like he was pushing back a non-existent hat. "My pleasure, ma'am."

I suppressed a giggle. It wasn't hard. I left Ted to show him the books while I walked back to the main office.

"Vince?" Cody said.

"Yeah."

"Why doesn't Detective Reed look at this Vince fellow?" Cody said. "I mean, he's the one who wants to keep men away from you."

"But Vince..." I stopped. Come to think of it, I did see him almost come to blows with an old man who had accidentally bumped him on the sidewalk. Vince had backed off; the old man was a former Marine and Vince was a chicken — I could see that now.

"You're right. I'll go back and suggest that." I set my mouth. "Hopefully, he'll take my suggestion." I walked back to the back room where Ted and Detective Reed were sitting.

There were three offices in back. Mine was to the left, and it was the biggest office. The doorway to the right actually led to one big room, which, at one point, was split into two smaller rooms. I was told that the back room once contained the coal for the furnace. It had been fixed up, obviously, since then, and contained a plywood bookcase and one of those ancient desks. I once saw an instruction book for the desk; it looked like it was from the nineteen-thirties.

Ted was sitting with Detective Reed. Not only did they have the current employee files, they looked like they had the whole drawer on my desk.

"That's a lot of files," I said. "Do you think you'll need all of those?"

"No, actually," Detective Reed said. "But it's better to have more information than not enough."

"Still." I made myself shut up. If Ted thought Reed

should see the files, I guess it was all right. I'd hate to sec-
ond-guess Ted at this point. At least, I should wait until
I've been here a month. Or two. "Cody had an interesting
idea."

"Yeah," Reed said, not looking up.

"He thought you should look into Vince's background."

"Are you sure that was Cody's idea?" Reed said.

Damn him! "Of course it was Cody's idea," I said
angrily. "You can ask him yourself."

I think my tone finally got through to Reed, because
he looked up at me. "Sorry. I didn't mean that the way it
came out."

I doubted that. I strode back to my office. Reed got
up and followed me. "What's Vince's last name, and
what's his address? I can see if he has a record."

I sighed. "I'll write it down for you." Angrily, I
wrote down his name, address, and phone number. And his
last workplace, which I suspected he had left. He never
kept a job long, and what was frustrating to me, he picked
up other jobs rather quickly.

"You remembered that rather handily."

"We were engaged for six months before I realized
what a creep the guy was."

"Are you sure that's his current address?"

"No," I said, "I'm not sure. I don't know if that's
his current employer, either, but that's where he was the
last time I updated anything on him." I shivered. "I'd rather
not think about him at all, but these things that have happened are..." Suspicious? Creepy? Distressing? All of the
above?

"Yes," he said, and he managed to look concerned.
"I can see your point." He got up. "I'll get out of your
hair."

I would have liked to have said "no problem," but it
was a problem, so I just nodded.

He went back to the other office, and I turned around to stare at the windows. For the first time, I realized that the blinds were opened. I shut them tight. That's all I needed—somebody to look at me through those windows.

So why did I feel so exposed?

CHAPTER 8

"I heard that Vince showed up this morning." Mom got up from her chair. I saw that she was dressed to go out.

"Who told you?" I said. "And where are we going?"

"I thought we might go to Kalamazoo." She looked me up and down. I was wearing a nice pair of pants, with a silk looking top. "We need to get a new wardrobe for you."

I looked down. "What's wrong with what I have on? I thought this one was all right."

"Nothing, actually," she held up a finger to forestall my comment, "if you're working in an accounting office."

"But," I objected, "I need to dress better than the salesmen in the office."

"Yes," she said, picking up her car keys, "But I told you -- not that much better. I'd like to get you some better blue jeans, perhaps some sturdier looking blouses. You want to relate to the contractors, even if you're not one of them."

"Jeans?" I said. "I haven't worn jeans to work since I was in college." I looked at her outfit. She was wearing nice slacks and a nice shirt. "You're dressed just like I am."

"Yes, but I'm not working there. I own the place." She started moving toward the car. "That's the difference. It's all in the image, Carrie."

"I still don't understand why *you* don't just take it over."

"I could," she agreed. "But. There's always a but. There would be this enormous believability problem. After so many years of being John's wife, without an outside career, do you think I could command anybody's respect? Except for being a hostess?"

"You have a point," I said, walking after her.

"Besides, your Father thought you had the potential to be a better leader than I could ever be."

"Daddy was an optimist."

She picked up her purse, sitting by the back door. "Daddy was a realist." She opened up the garage door, and I gasped.

There was Vince.

"What are you doing here?"

"I wanted to talk to you without that madman sticking a gun in my face. Baby, I just want to talk."

"We talked a long time ago," I said. "Go away before I call the police."

"Your boyfriend went home a long time ago."

I laughed. "Stetson Reed? My boyfriend? He's investigating a murder."

"I'm sure he's just there to be around you."

I rolled my eyes. "I'm calling the police. And then I'm getting a protection order."

"But," he said, "I just wanted to talk, baby. Can't you just talk to me? I miss you so much. We were good for each other."

And other clichés. Right. "I'm calling the police."

"Too late," Mom said, appearing in the kitchen doorway. "I've already called them." She waved a phone. Bless her. "So I suggest you leave my property before they come."

"Okay, okay," he said. "Jeez." He walked off.

"Are you sure we should leave the house?"

"Oh," Mom said. "Didn't I tell you about Bruno?" We got into the car and she started to back out of the drive.

"Bruno?"

She pressed a button inside the door. Inside the house, a large dog started to bark. I looked at her, questioningly.

"It was our new alarm we just installed. If someone knocks on the door when we're not there, 'Bruno' will start barking." She smiled. "And if they call my bluff, they still have to get past the security system."

Now that I remembered. Mom and Dad had in-stalled a security system some years ago. I even remembered the security code, since it was an anagram of my birthday. "Nice idea, Mom."

"We," and her face fell. "We thought it was." She fell silent as she drove down the street.

I chewed my bottom lip. "And it still is, Mom," I said, tears threatening to fall.

She smiled. "Let's go get you some outfits."

<<<<>>>>

We ended up with a pair of dark blue jeans, some brown and gray slacks, suitable for outside wear, a couple of cardigans, and a couple of plain white button-down shirts and a couple of neutral color shirts. We also ended up with a couple of leather shoes and a nice pair of sturdy boots to tromp out in the yard. When I objected to the cost, Mom said that I could pay her back.

But, when I admired a nice dress, Mom picked that one up, too, in her "to-buy" pile. "Mom!" I said, in the dressing room. "I was just trying it on! Where would I wear it?"

"Oh, I don't know. You need a nice dress to wear someplace, I think. Maybe on a date?" She suggested the last with a smile.

"Mom! I don't even have a boyfriend." I started to take the dress off to put it back on the hanger.

She grabbed the dress. "Not yet," she said calmly. "I know I won't have any grandchildren, but I would like to see you settled before I die." She took the dress from me.

I shivered. "Mom! You're going to live for a long time!"

"You never know, honey," she said, with a far-off look in her eyes. "I thought your Dad would outlive me. I would have sworn that on a Bible."

She was definitely having a down day. "I know, Mom." I shrugged on my blouse and looked her in the eye.

"Let's go get something to eat. Food court?"

"Sounds good to me."

One thing about Mom. In one minute, she'll spend hundreds of dollars on my clothing — which I don't deserve, by the way, and I fully intend to pay her back — the next minute, we're eating in the Food Court because it's cheaper than a restaurant. She has no problems with the McDonald's of the world, as long as she can get her senior coffee free. We went up the escalator to the food court—

-- and almost ran into Detective Stetson. I blinked at him. "What are you doing here?"

His eyebrows lowered. "It's a free country."

"Carrie!" Mom said. "The proper greeting is 'Hello! It's nice to see you!'" She shook her head at me. "May I call you Stetson?" she said.

He smiled at her. "Actually, I'd rather you didn't, Mrs. Burton. I've always hated that name." He held out his hand. "Call me Andy."

"Andy?" I said. "How did you..."

"Stetson Andrew Reed," he explained. "Some people use my first name; some use my middle. I answer to both."

"Will you join us for lunch?" Mom said. "And — please call me Marie."

"I shouldn't," he said apologetically and with a smile. "You're technically both still suspects."

"Really," I said.

"You're both suspects," he said, "but you're not in my personal top ten."

I started moving on, towards the Food Court. "Gee, you have no idea how warm and cozy that makes me feel."

"I'm sorry," he said.

"I doubt it," I said.

"Carrie!" Mom said. "Andy is going to eat with us, and that's that. No talking of murder at the table, unless it's sports."

He grinned. "Are you a Lions fan?"

"Sort of," she grinned back. "I've developed an appreciation for football after watching it with my husband all of these years."

My eyebrows moved together. I didn't know that. Usually, she left the room for the other TV when football was on. Maybe things had changed.

"So what do you think about the season?" Mom and Detective Reed — I refused to call him Andy — walked off, talking, and left me to follow, carrying the bags. They chattered about football during lunch, while I picked through my sweet and sour chicken.

Finally, they wound down and we all looked at each other. "So," Mom said, "why don't we see you in church anymore?"

His face turned serious. "To be honest, Marie, by the time I get to Sunday, I'm so physically and mentally tired that church has no appeal for me."

"I've always found that it invigorates me," Mom said. "Especially listening to the Anthems."

"Maybe I should try it again," Detective Reed said. "But I probably should wait until the investigation is over."

"But," Mom said, "that could be weeks."

Detective Reed inclined his head. "True."

"Okay," she said. "Here's a thought. Don't some of your suspects go to church?"

He grinned. "Yeah."

"So go to church to observe your suspects. Stay for the sermon."

I snorted. He grinned. "Well, that's the most unusual reason to come back to church that I've ever heard."

"Works, doesn't it?"

Still smiling, I looked at the other end of the food court. There was Vince, looking at us. He was frowning. "Don't look now, but Vince is looking at us."

Detective Reed's smile dropped. "Where?"

"At the other end."

He started to turn his head. I touched his hand. "Don't look."

"Do you suppose he followed you here?" Mom said.

I shrugged. "I hope not."

"Well," Reed said, "this is a public place, and you don't have a protection order against him yet." He glanced over toward Vince casually. "Has he ever threatened you? Has he ever hit you?" He hesitated. "I know he grabbed your arm, but besides that."

"No."

"We can't put a protection order on a guy because he creeps you out."

"I wasn't asking you to."

He bit his lip. "I didn't mean that the way it came out."

"For a detective," I said, "you sure have a lot of slips of the lip."

He glared at me.

"Carrie, I'm sure that Andy only has your best interests in mind."

"Of course," Detective Reed said. He didn't exactly look penitent.

"In the meantime," Mom said. "Let's part friends. Even if we have to do this for show." She looked at me. "I think we were done shopping, anyway. Can you walk us out, to make sure that Vince doesn't follow us?"

"I think," Reed said, "that I should follow you home."

"Oh, I don't think that's necessary," I said. "Like you said, Vince hasn't been violent, and I can't let a creep get to me."

"Do you have your shopping done?" Mom said.

"No, actually. I was going to find a new winter coat."

"Let's help you. Maybe we'll bore Vince to death."

"Right," I said.

"It'll be fun. I used to help..." her face fell. "I used to help your father shop." She put her game face back on. "Come on." She got up. "Where were you going?"

"Oh, just to the shop down there." He pointed.

So we followed Detective Reed down the mall. Every so often, I caught sight of Vince, but finally, I hadn't seen him for about a half an hour. "I think he's gone," I said.

"Let me buy you a drink," Detective Reed said, "and we'll make sure."

"A drink?" I said, my eyebrows going up.

"A pop," he clarified. "From the food court. To thank you for your input."

"Are you sure you want to buy something for a suspect?"

He snorted. "Like I said, you two are *way* down on my suspect list."

So we went back to the Food Court and bought a couple of drinks.

This time, we saw John and Elinor Logan and invited them over. I hadn't thought they got out of town much, but here they were. "Stetson," John said, shaking his hand, "it's good to see you again."

"Mr. Logan. Mrs. Logan."

"Stetson used to work for us at the Hardware store," he said. "Before he went off to college and got all of that police training."

"Yeah?" I said. "You know," I turned to Stetson, "you surprise me all the time. So, you know a socket wrench from a ply bar?" Actually, I was just introduced to a socket wrench, myself, this past week.

"The last I looked, yes. But a socket wrench is usually used on engines, not in lumberyards." He looked at me. "Why do you have socket wrenches?"

Good question.

"Why not?" I shrugged.

"He was a good worker," Mr. Logan said. "If he hadn't gone into the police force, I would have been happy to hire him back."

"Why *did* you come back to town?" I said. "It strikes me that going back among people who you know, and who know you, could be a conflict of interest."

"On the other hand, because I do know how they think," he said, "that could also be a benefit."

"Yet," I countered, "they know your weak spots."

"And I know theirs."

He stared at me, and again I noticed those intense blue eyes. In spite of my annoyance, he did have beautiful eyes. And quite a nice face. His gaze turned distant. "I also had a personal reason," he said slowly, "for coming back." He turned away.

Mom kicked my shin.

I glanced at her. She shook her head slightly. Okay, I was going to have to hear about this later. It must have been after I left for college, because I didn't remember hearing anything about the Reed family.

I took a sip of coke. "I'm getting a little tired," Mom said. "I think it's about time we drive home. Don't you, Carrie?"

"Yeah," I said, standing up. "It was a pleasure to see you again," I said, turning to the Logans. "Detective Reed."

He turned back. "I'll follow you home."

Mom nodded. "That would be nice of you," she said, laying her hand on Detective Reed's arm.

"He's probably gone," I said.

"But, if he isn't, having Andy follow us home won't hurt."

I nodded.

As soon as we were in the car, Mom started. "I

don't understand why you keep insulting Andy."

"Because he thinks we're suspects to a murder of a little old man. He also annoys me a lot."

"But," she looked at me sideways, "he's still a good-looking man, right?"

"Well, yeah," I said, still thinking of how annoying he was. "Wait, what?"

"Never mind."

"Well, yes, he is good looking," I said. "What does that have to do with anything?"

"Nothing." Mom made a left turn. I looked behind us. Detective Reed's blue Chevy truck was following behind us at a discrete distance.

"Don't speed," I said. "He'll pick you up for speeding."

"I never speed," Mom said. "Well, not when the police are following me."

"So," I said. "Why did you kick me?"

"Oh, yes." She was silent for a moment. "Did you ever know the Reeds?"

"No, I don't think so."

"This was after you left for college. Andy was a senior in high school. He came home from school one day to find both of his parents murdered and his house ransacked.

"Oh, my God," I said. Chills went down my spine. I couldn't imagine finding my parents murdered. It was sad enough about old Joe, much less somebody I actually knew.

"He was cleared; they were murdered at lunch and he was seen at school all day."

"Did they find out who — "

"No. I don't think that Andy knew what he was going to do before that, but after that, well..."

I exhaled. He had two possible reactions to something like that — trying to find the murderers or getting out of town and never coming back. He chose the first. I wouldn't have blamed him if he hadn't come back, but facing the problem head on made his character rise up in my estimation.

"Has he had any breakthroughs?"

"Not that I ever heard. That was years ago; the cold case is glacial by now. He may never find out who did the murder." Mom looked sad. "I remember Mrs. Reed. We didn't run in the same circles, but I remember they were very nice."

"I thought you knew everybody in town?" I grinned.

"Some more than others," she responded. "It only seems like I know everybody. There are still a few people in the county I don't know."

I snickered.

"Now you're feeling better." Mom was silent for a few minutes. "Look, I know you're going to have to deal with Andy until we find out who murdered old Joe. I'm just telling you that he's really not that bad."

"I know, I know." I said. "And I'm sad for him. He just—annoys me."

"Get over it," Mom said sharply. "Andy is not your enemy. After all, he didn't have to follow us home to keep us safe from Vince."

"True."

We were silent for the rest of the ride home. We drove into the garage. Detective Reed honked at us, Mom waved at him and closed the door.

I kept listening for a knock on the door from Vince the rest of the night. When I finally went to sleep, I dreamt of Detective Reed's blue eyes.

106

CHAPTER 9

I looked at myself in the mirror in my bedroom. Black was not a good look with my blonde hair, but, since Mom was paying for the funeral, she insisted that we be the "family" of the deceased. Personally, I'd rather let dung beetles crawl all over my body then go to a funeral home, especially one with an open casket, which, of course, this would be. So, what does one wear with black?

I had thought sincerely of wearing a bright red blouse, but not only did I not think I'd get it past my Mom, I definitely wouldn't get it past Mrs. Grundy. And, since I was now a respected businesswoman, I didn't dare offend the good ladies of this town, because they gossiped to their husbands, and the husbands buy from the lumberyard.

And ladies didn't? I laughed ironically. I was glad to laugh, I suspect I would be misty eyed before the day was finished.

"Are you ready, Carrie?"

"Just a second." I grabbed my eye shadow and put a little on. Normally, I used lighter makeup, but this occasion seemed to call for a greater effort.

With what I was doing, I was beginning to wonder whether I was going to a visitation or a coming out party.

I sighed and pushed open the bathroom, put on a pair of heels, and walked downstairs. Mom was dressed in a black skirt, black pantyhose, and a white blouse with a long black pearl-like necklace. She looked gorgeous. I only wish I looked like her at sixty-something.

She looked me over top to bottom. "Very nice."

"Can I go to the prom, Mom?"

She smiled, a little sadly. "I don't want to go, either. It feels like we just spent an eternity there."

"We did." I went to the closet to pick up my coat. "I think Austin's should name a wing in our name."

"You think?" She smiled. "Daddy would have liked that joke."

"He would have taken off with it and told them that we should name the whole building after him."

"True." She looked at her watch. "We have to go."

Because we were "family," we were early, along with the Logans. We invited the residents of the Foster Care to come, but Ellen didn't think that most of them could handle it. But we did pick up Ashley, and the other residents would come later.

As we approached the home, Ashley looked out the window. "I don't want to go there," she said.

"Why, Ashley?" Mom asked gently. "We need to say goodbye to our friend, Joe."

She crossed her arms. "I don't like to say goodbye."

"Why, Ashley?" I said.

"'Cause every time I say goodbye in that place, I never see them again." She shivered. "And they're always so cold when I touch them."

"That's because they've passed away."

She nodded. "They're in heaven. And I know that I'll go there someday, but not yet."

I glanced back at her. It was amazing that we were the same age, more or less, because I would have expected to hear these questions from a child.

Mom pulled in and parked. "Do you believe in heaven, Ashley?"

108

She nodded. "But I haven't been there."

"There are very few people here that have."

"But what if he's gone to the other place? He always told me that he'd probably go to the other place — underground."

"Oh, no, Ashley, I don't think he's gone to the other place," Mom said. "I saw him do a lot of good deeds."

Really, Mom? He looked crazy to me.

But Ashley was nodding. "He used to help me with the folding and my coloring and all sorts of stuff. Even though he said crazy stuff."

"See?"

"But I don't want to see him."

"You can stay in the other room," Mom said, "and say hello to all of the people who walk in."

"Do you think there's going to be a lot?" I said, quietly.

"You might be surprised. Curiosity goes a long way in this town."

"Do you think that the perp will show up?"

"Perp?" Ashley said. She looked vaguely alarmed. Maybe she watched some cop shows.

Mom and I looked at each other. "Just our joke," I said lamely. I wasn't sure how much she had been told.

"Okay," She started to get out of the car. Quickly, Mom and I got out of the car and went after her. We caught up with her at the door. Gabe Austin, the undertaker's son, met us.

"Let me take your coats, and you can leave your purses in our office."

"Thank you." I did a double take. This young man hadn't been here the last few weeks, and I hadn't made the connection before. "Were you the little kid who lived down the street from us?"

109

He grinned. "No, you were the big kid who lived down the street from me."

"Why didn't I see you a couple of weeks ago?" I said.

"Mid-winter break. Home from college," he said.

I blinked. "You're going to school?"

"After rebelling against my Dad's business for a few years," he said, "I decided I was ready to settle down and learn the business."

"Like me," I sighed.

He grimaced. "Yeah. Like you. I'm sorry for your loss."

"Thank you," I said. I handed him my coat, and we went in to see Joe.

Laid out in his coffin, old Joe had a quiet dignity he hadn't had in life. I gazed down at him. The embalming process had smoothed out some of his wrinkles, and behind the death mask, I could see the remnants of the handsome man he used to be. What a darned shame, his whole life. To have his mind taken from him at a young age because of violence, and then his life taken in violence. I prayed that he would find peace in his afterlife.

What a shame he thought he would go to hell.

I moved onward. The Logans had brought a photo album. I looked at the pictures of a handsome young man with dark hair. He was looking tenderly down at a fair-haired woman holding a baby in a christening gown, who was staring at the couple, as if she couldn't believe what was above her. I smiled at the baby and wished that they could find the wife or the child.

Mom was leading a reluctant Ashley to the coffin. "He's not going to hurt you."

Ashley looked indignant. "He never hurt me. But I don't want to see him." She glanced at him, then shut her eyes. Then she opened her eyes and stared at him. "He looks nice." She looked at Mom. "He's in a suit. I never saw him in a suit."

Mom had bought that, too. She said it was undignified to bury a vet in the rags he had been wearing.

Ashley looked at the flag on the coffin. "Why's that there?"

"He's a veteran, dear," Mom said.

I blinked. He was a war veteran, wasn't he? Which made it even more amazing that he had no defensive wounds when I found him. I thought back to the hand I saw sticking out of the bottom of number three. No. I was told that he had been stabbed, numerous times, but his hands and forearms were unmarked.

That made no sense.

Daddy had been in Vietnam, and, like most veterans, had never talked of his experience. But one thing I learned early on is that you never touched him to wake him up. He came up swinging.

Those guys were trained to fight without thinking.

I looked back at Joe. Why hadn't he fought? Was he dead before he was stabbed? I hadn't seen the coroner's report, of course, but when I saw those wounds, I doubted it. His clothes were covered in blood.

Was it somebody he knew and trusted?

Was it a complete stranger?

I was going to have to keep my eyes open tonight. Would a murderer come to a funeral home to view his victim?

Perhaps. If he hadn't gotten what he wanted.

But what could he learn from a corpse?

Maybe nothing. Maybe I was overthinking it, and it was just a random act of violence to a little old man.

Then why did they dump him in barn number three?

I realized that I had been staring down at Joe for a long time, and I moved to find my Mom. She was greeting the Logans, and I moved over by her side.

"Well," Mr. Logan said. He glanced over at the coffin. "I knew this would happen someday, but I figure he would die in his sleep, not stabbed to death."

My thoughts, exactly.

"Can you think of why he wouldn't defend himself?" I said.

Mr. Logan shook his head. "I'm not sure what was going on in his head."

"Why did he call people 'squire'?"

Mr. Logan smiled. "That I can answer. He had a fascination with England when he was a kid. He was probably flashing back."

"Yeah, probably," I said.

Ashley had wandered out to the front room. "Hello," she said brightly.

"I think I had better follow her." I wandered out to the front room.

She was shaking the hand of a middle-aged couple. So much for my tasteful black and white outfit, this woman was dressed in the loudest muumuu I had ever seen. Blue clashed with yellow, clashed with red, clashed with some indeterminate color. It looked as if the color palette was having a battle. I approached them. "Are you here for Joe?"

"Yes," the woman said. "What a shame. That

little old man."

"I know," I said. "Hi. I'm Carrie Burton."

She smiled. "Yes, I know. I met you at your father's funeral."

My smile fell. "I'm sorry, I don't remember. I'm afraid that day was a big blur."

"I'm Mary McBride," she said. "And this is my husband, Larry."

The small man, dressed in black pants and a button up white shirt, murmured hello to the ground. I wondered if I would hear another word out of him that night.

"Well," she said, "we should see the body." I decided I should stay with Ashley. I didn't think I could stand listening to them standing over the body and saying how natural he looked.

I heard that enough a couple of weeks ago. Only that time, they were standing over my Dad. I wanted to scream at people like that. He's dead! What do you think he's going to look like? It's not like we're going to exhibit him covered with mold!

Sometimes, my mind does some weird things.

I stared after the couple. I had avoided funerals most of my life; this experience wasn't helping.

The next pair that came were two men. I recognized them as contractors. "Hi, guys!" I approached them, and they looked up at me. For a moment, I don't think they recognized me. "Oh, hello, Miss Burton."

"Call me Carrie," I said. "I'm guess I'm surprised to see you here."

One of the guys looked at the other. "Why? We knew old Squire."

I felt a little abashed. "I'm sorry; I haven't been home very long. I don't know who knows who in this town yet."

The other man grinned. "I know the feeling."

I cocked my head. "Do I know you from someplace else?"

He rolled his eyes. "Yeah. You do. We graduated together. Mike Deland?"

My mind did a mental flip. I remembered a little tiny guy named Mike, but, as I looked up at this tall man, I realized that he was right. I mean, he was Mike. "Oh, my God. You grew!"

He grinned. "A foot after I turned eighteen."

"Married?"

He showed off his ring. "To an out-of-town girl. Her name is Dana. Three kids."

"Cool!" I grinned ruefully. "I never married."

"Which surprises me," Mike said. "You were a popular girl in school."

"Bad choice in men, then the last one was a toad." I looked at the door. Sure enough, Vince had walked in. "That one. He's a stalker."

Mike raised his eyebrows. "Then what's he doing here?"

"That's what I'd like to know. He didn't know Joe; he didn't even live in this town." I strode up to Vince, followed by Mike.

"What are you doing here, Vince?" Did the man ever wash his hair? I sniffed discreetly. As a matter of fact, did he ever clean himself?

"It's a free country," he muttered.

"It is," I agreed, "so I have a right not to want to see your face ever again." I sighed. "Vince," I said, "you may go in and pay your respects to the deceased and then I want you out of here." Mike stood beside me. I could see out the corner of my eye that he was attempting to look as fierce as possible. To my eyes, he wasn't very successful, but

114

Vince gulped as he looked up at him.

He moved into the room where Joe lay, stood looking at the old man, glanced at the flowers, walked past Mom, who stared at him, then walked past me, giving me a glare.

I sagged a little as he left. Mom gave me a quick look, and I gave her a thumbs up. She went back to talking to the Logans and another couple who had come in while I was talking to Vince.

I started to mingle after that. With the people wandering around, about all we needed was some champagne and finger food, and we would have a rollicking party. Mr. Logan sidled up beside me. "Joe would have enjoyed this," he said quietly. "Before and after the war, he always liked a good wake."

"But it seems so... disrespectful," I muttered back.

He smiled. "Ah, but you're still young." He looked at Joe. "I'm in no hurry to leave this earth, but in some ways, I envy him now."

"I don't."

"I don't expect you to."

"We still need to find his murderer." I gazed over the crowd, wondering whether his murderer was in this room, or whether it was, truly, a random act of violence, and his murderer was long gone from this town.

"Do you think you'll find him or her here?"

I shrugged. "I don't know. But at least I can try."

"True." He wandered off. I went to the outer room. I had seen Ted and James earlier. Cody was just walking in and had signed the register. "Cody! Hi. I wasn't sure you would come."

"I thought I should give him my respects."

Cody finished signing.

I saw some tension in his face. "Do you hate these things, too?"

"With a passion," he said tersely. "But I thought I should come."

"That was nice of you," I said. "Do you want to see the body?"

"Yes. And no."

"I know how you feel. Let me go in with you." I walked in with him and through the crowd. He didn't look at anyone else, but he was focused on the body. When we reached the coffin, he stared down at it for a long minute, then closed his eyes. I thought I saw an odd expression on his face, but it was gone so quickly, I doubted whether I saw anything.

He turned away, then caught sight of the photo album. He seemed transfixed by the picture of Joe, his wife, and the baby. "Seems odd that he had children," I said. "You know?"

"Yeah. I know." He glanced back at the body. "I hope I never turn old like that."

"I think we all hope that we don't end up that way," I said. "But it's not in our hands."

"Sometimes it is," he started, then stopped. "Medical things, you know," he finally continued.

"I know what you mean," I said. "Well, I have to mingle again." I moved off, then spotted Ted at the door. "Hi, Ted."

He looked around. "Quite a turn-out." He said. "I suppose some of them are curiosity seekers."

"Yeah," I said. "I figured."

"Is your Mom here... Oh, I see her."

"Cody and Jimmy have been here," I said. "I just left Cody."

"Cody?" Ted said. "I'm surprised. He hates these places."

I smiled. "So do I. Maybe he felt he had to come."

"Have you seen Matt?"

"Not yet." I moved closer. "Do you think Sam will come?"

Ted snorted. "Not likely. You've seen how anti-social he can be."

"I need to ask you what his problem is," I said. "But later. Not here."

Ted frowned. "Don't take this personally, but it's you."

"I didn't do anything to him."

Ted shrugged. "You're female. That's enough. Trust me, I've heard his talk about female managers."

"Misogynist?"

"Slightly. I think he has no problem with female managers as long as they don't try to manage him."

I rolled my eyes. "Oh, great. There's not much I can do about my gender."

"But your gender does have an impact."

"It does?"

"It's a small town. You'll see." He looked around. "I'd like to talk to your mother."

"About me?" I grinned.

It was his turn to roll his eyes. "Yeah. I'm going to put in for a male manager." He smiled widely to show that he was kidding.

I smiled back. "You had *better* smile while you say that." He moved off.

I looked around the room. I finally spotted Ashley by the coffin. She was, once again, staring down at Joe. Tears dripped off the end of her nose. I

117

moved beside her and gave her a hug. "He was a good man," she sniffled into my shoulder.

"I barely knew him," I told her. "Can you tell me about him?"

"He liked fried chicken," she said. "He liked to walk around town and sell newspapers. He liked to take naps in the afternoon. When I cried, he gave me hugs and called me Joanna."

"Joanna?" I interrupted.

"Ellen told me that his daughter was named Joanna."

"I wonder... Oh, because you were young, like his daughter was." Or seemed young. Because she had the mental age of a child, she probably appealed to him as a child. "What else?"

"He helped me with my coloring," she said. "He helped me wash dishes, even though he yelled at me when I dropped a glass."

"Was it loud?" *Like a gunshot*, I thought.

"Yeah."

"What did he used to say?"

She smiled. "He called people 'squire.' That made me laugh. He liked walking to the lumber yard."

Not exactly what I asked — I was thinking of the dropped glass — but I would take it. "Did you know why he walked to the lumberyard?"

"He said he was visiting Grandpa."

I frowned. "OK." Hum.

She thought. "He wore Old Spice that tickled my nose."

"Now, see?" I said. "He's not totally gone, is he?"

"I guess not." She glanced at Joe. "I think I'm going out there." She pointed at the outer room, then got up and shuffled out. She started greeting people coming in. Most people smiled at her, some clearly avoided her.

I suppressed a sigh. I wished I could go out there.

From recent experience, I knew that we shouldn't leave until the last guest had left. I saw a ton of people that evening, but, quite frankly, didn't see anybody act suspicious like I thought they might. "Well," I said after we finally dropped Ashley off, "that was a bust."

Mom smiled tiredly. "Oh, I don't know," she said. "I heard a lot about the Newton family. You knew that they once owned the land the lumberyard was on, right?"

"Oh. Yes, I did. I had forgotten." That would explain why Joe thought he was visiting his grandfather.

"The rumor was that there was a treasure buried there once."

I screwed up my face. "You're kidding."

"Yeah. One day, almost eighty years ago, the family came out of their house to find the yard full of holes. One of the neighbors had come over in the night and had tried to dig up their supposed treasure. They laughed him off their land, telling him that all of their money was in the bank, where it should be."

I grinned. "So they didn't bury their money in their backyard in a jar?"

"Nothing was ever found," she said. "You know, most of that yard has been dug up since then to place buildings and so forth. Even if there were a treasure, I'm sure someone would have found it by now."

"I would have thought so," I said. I rubbed my hands together. "Anyway, after all of these years, why would anybody think that Joe would re-member anything?"

"Times are desperate," Mom said. "Who knows? Maybe it's some meth addict."

"Yeah," I said. But I couldn't rid myself of the feeling that it was still a murder by someone he didn't even try to defend himself against. Someone he trusted. Someone he thought he knew.

CHAPTER 10

The funeral the next day was almost anti-climactic, if rather interesting. The rest of the foster care home came that day, and a couple of the residents kept trying to leave the funeral home. Finally, young Austin placed a "guard" at the door, keeping those two from leaving. They weren't noisy about it, but it was still a bit distracting, just the same.

The lumber yard was open that day, but Ted and I sneaked out and met my mother. We figured that was the best thing to do, considering poor Joe was dumped on our property.

When the minister asked if anyone would like to say a word, Ted surprised me by standing up. "I have to admit," he said, standing up at the podium and looking out at the relatively small crowd, "that I didn't know Joe like some of you did. I only heard what he was like before the war. He was a kind man. He was a husband and a father. He was a young man with a promising career in accounting— "

I blinked, startled. Accounting?

"—when he gave all that up and volunteered to help fight the threats from Hitler and Nazi Germany. He served honorably, as long as he was able, but the fight grew to be too much for him. While his body went on living, most of his spirit was killed in Germany, never to return." He paused. "Oh, sometimes we saw glimpses of what he used to be. I recall one time when he walked into our offices — into my office — looked over my shoulder at our books, and before I could shoo him out, he told me where my math was wrong. And, of course, he was right."

I looked around. People were smiling.

"He also helped various people."

Ashley popped up, smiling. "Joe helped me!" she

said loudly.

"He didn't have the life that he expected to live, but this town is a little poorer from losing him. May his soul be healed in the loving arms of Jesus."

A couple of people sniffed loudly. I wiped my nose. When Ted sat down, I leaned over him. "Very nice."

Ted smiled sadly. "I've had too much practice lately."

My smile fell. "Oh. Right."

"Is there anyone else?"

Detective Reed strode up the aisle, startling me. I hadn't seen him come in; I guess I hadn't expected him to come. "I, also, saw glimpses of the old Joe. I used to help him around town, giving him rides, and he would help me balance my checkbook." He smiled.

A titter rippled through the church.

"I just wanted the community to know that I vow to find his killer, no matter how long it takes me."

Turning to the coffin, he saluted it smartly, then strode back to his seat. I smiled at him, but he was looking the other way and ignored me.

Mr. Logan stood up. "Joe and I were best friends. And I'm not sure most of the community knew this, but I was his guardian." His voice quavered. "He and I were the same age, so I saw him grow up from a freckle faced kid to the old man we both became. And, in that time, while many times he was a stranger to the real world, preferring to live in his own world, his personality never truly changed. While he was trained to fight in the war, he was never truly a violent man, which makes what happened to him so puzzling.

"I know that I will soon join him in the great beyond and we will laugh over our lives. But until then, I will miss my friend."

He moved unsteadily down the aisle and sat next to his wife, who patted his arm.

I looked around while the minister called for more participants. Did anyone look guilty? Was there anyone there who shouldn't be there?

If there was a murderer there at the funeral, I, for one, couldn't spot him. Or her.

The funeral finally got over. An honor guard took the flag from his coffin, folded it, and offered it to my Mom. She waved it off, offering it to Mrs. Logan. Mrs. Logan shook her head. The guard stood, not sure what to do, when Mrs. Logan got up and pulled Ashley forward. The guard gave the flag to Ashley, and I think I had never seen a happier face in my life.

We exited the church, getting ready to drive to the cemetery. Fortunately, his parents had bought a third lot, and he was to be buried next to them. As I was walking out, one of the Herculaneum trucks drove by slowly. I recognized Cody in the driver's seat. He saw me, nodded, then turned right onto Main Street.

What was he doing here? Must be coincidence — maybe somebody had a delivery. Still, that left Jimmy, Mathew, and Sam to run the lumberyard. I turned to Ted. "Did you see Cody?"

"Yeah."

"Think we need to get back?"

Mom overheard. "You two are staying right here," she said decisively. "We still need to put a show on for Mrs. Grundy."

Ted glanced at her. "Mrs. Grundy?"

"The gossips in town," I whispered, and he smiled slightly.

We traveled slowly to the cemetery. The Logans drove behind us, and we drove behind the hearse — the converted mini-van the Austins were using. We passed by the lumberyard. As we passed, the guys and Cody — he must have gotten back — stood in the front and saluted as the funeral went by. I turned to Mom. "Did you get them to do that?"

"No," she said honestly. "But that was a good idea. Was it yours, Ted?"

"No. But I bet it was Jimmy's. He was a Vietnam War Vet, you know."

No. I didn't know. "Mom," I said, "do we have to do everything for Mrs. Grundy? Someday, I might want to break loose, get drunk or something."

"Carrie." She hesitated. "Just make sure you do it away from town."

I rolled my eyes.

The graveside services were, mercifully, short. We left the coffin there to be interred. I could see the cemetery workers waiting impatiently along the side. "So, back to the church?" I said.

"Yeah," she said. Mom was starting to look tired. "I'll be glad when this day is over." We started walking back to the car when a man came up from the side. I saw Mom's lip compress. "Mr. Collingsworth."

Oh. So that was Mike Collingsworth. I tried to stare at him surreptitiously. He was tall, thin, with a hawk-like nose and sharp brown eyes. His black hair was touched with silver. In spite of this rather alarming appearance — after all, somebody like this shouldn't wear black — his baritone voice was warm. I wondered if he didn't charm the birds from the trees.

"Mrs. Burton," he said. "I've never had the opportunity to tell you how sorry I was when I heard about your husband."

Mom allowed him to take her hand. "Thank you."

"I just wanted to let you know that my offer still stands."

"I appreciate your concern," Mom said. Her voice was rather tinged with irony. "But I plan to keep the lumberyard."

He shook his head. "Are you sure you want the

124

trouble?"

Mom's voice turned sharp, and she glanced back at the lonely coffin on its stand. "Are you referring to —"she stopped.

"No. No!" He looked shocked, but his eyes narrowed. "But now that you mention it..."

"I realize that our yard is not in the best part of town anymore, but, after all, it's not like we're going to move."

"I'm not suggesting that you move."

"No," she said dryly. "You're just suggesting that we sell."

"I don't understand," I said, "why you want so badly to buy the lumberyard."

He shrugged. "I don't want to see it closed."

Mom snorted.

"Okay, I said, "you don't want to see it closed. We're not planning on closing it. So you should be happy."

He looked at me. "But you can't run it."

"Why?" My voice was getting louder. "Because I'm a woman?"

"Exactly!"

"Really?" Ted had walked up behind us and stood there, listening. I glanced at him and went on. "The last time I looked, it was the twenty-first century. Women don't necessarily stay home and tend to their kitchens and have supper and a pipe ready for their husbands. They're out there working, fighting wars, and being mechanics. There's no reason not to have lady lumberyard owners or contractors or whatever they want to be."

Mr. Collingsworth seemed taken aback. "Okay, you can run it. But why would you want to?" He started to walk away. "Just don't be surprised if bad things happen."

Detective Reed had walked into earshot and raised his eyebrows. "Mr. Collingsworth," he said dangerously, "I would suggest you not make statements like that around the police. Especially around policemen who are investigating a murder." He looked him up and down, as if measuring him for handcuffs and an orange outfit. "Because that sounded a lot like a threat."

Mike Collingsworth managed to look innocent. "Who said anything about threats? You know, as I know, that the yard is not in a good part of town."

"Uh-huh." Reed gave him another look. He pulled an evidence bag out of his pocket — it looked like one of those DNA thingies — and looked speculatively at Collingsworth. Mike looked at him and quickly walked away.

I started laughing. I couldn't help it.

"Well," Mom said, "I guess we won't see *him* at the luncheon."

Reed chuckled. For a moment, I actually liked him. For the moment.

CHAPTER 11

The next two days were uneventful. Thank God. They were cold, but clear, and Ted finally took me on the tour of the yard. I listened dutifully, but I knew that I would forget everything unless it was drummed into me. I vowed to walk in the yard every day, exploring, until I got a feel for the inventory. One of the jobs of being a president was to try to be on top of everything, even if one wasn't the expert. I certainly wasn't the expert in buying lumber.

I learned the difference between number one and number four boards, the difference between AB grade and CD grade of plywood, and the difference between plywood and oriented strand board and what each was used for. And then I discovered something. I loved the smell of fresh-sawn wood. Well, okay, I wasn't going to wear the scent behind my ears, although that certainly might attract some men, but a bit of fresh-sawn pine smelled almost as good as chocolate brownies.

Maybe it smelled so good because now my income depended on it?

In the meantime, I started to make arrangements to move back to town. I was going to move in with my mother until neither of us could stand it anymore, or at least until I got my footing again. All of my furniture — which was old, anyway — was going to Goodwill, and I was going to buy a new bed and dresser for my bedroom. After all, my room still had posters of Patrick Swayze and Pierce Brosnan on the walls. A forty-something year old should have more refined tastes, right?

But I rolled the posters up carefully and put them in a tube in the back of my closet so that I could drool at them every once in a while.

I was going to move myself, but while I was at

work one day, Mom called around to the moving companies and arranged for one of those who do everything. I fussed at her when I got home that night. "Mom. I can't afford that!"

"Yes," she said, not looking up from the purple mittens she was making for the church bazaar. "Not only can you afford that now, I'm paying for it."

"Mo—om! You've already bought new outfits for me *and* paid for a funeral." I sounded whiny, even to me. What is it about Mothers that turn full-grown adults into fifteen-year-olds? "Can you afford...?"

"Yes," she said, definitively.

I had never thought about it, because I hadn't quite made the connection between lumber yard profits and my parents' income. And I hadn't actually done a payroll yet. But when Mom was as resolute as she was right then, knitting those mittens, I knew there was no arguing with her.

When I finally did a payroll a couple of days later— crying a little over Daddy's last check—I sat and thought. Their spending never was extravagant, and the payroll combined with the very, very few draws they made seemed to add up to quite a bit.

Yes, she could afford it.

So that was settled. I had planned to go back to the apartment that weekend and move the few things that I didn't trust any mover to package correctly, but then Detective Stetson Reed walked back into my life and my office. To be honest, I had wondered whether anything was coming of the investigation, but I had been busy at work, and, after the little talk with Ted about Reed, I wasn't anxious to meet Stetson again.

I was just settling into a routine. I was looking at newer computer software and hardware — I knew what the accounting office I had worked at used, but I knew that a small lumber company was definitely not going to pay thousands of dollars for software. So I was looking at the cheaper programs. I realized subconsciously that someone was at my door, but I thought they might have been looking at shingle samples. I looked up when I heard a tiny knock on the door jamb.

I looked up and smiled. Detective Reed glowered at me. I was about to ask him how the case was going, but the question died under that glare. "Yes?" I said, efficiently, but with a sinking feeling that he looked like trouble.

"Why didn't you tell me you had a felon on staff?"

I looked blank. I had looked through the employee records, but I hadn't noticed anything like that.

"I do?" I said, acting dumb. It wasn't hard; I had no idea what he was talking about. "Who?" My bets, quite frankly, were on Sam Kline. Two weeks later, and he could still barely bring himself to look at me.

"Me," Cody said, appearing at the door.

I blinked at him. "Really?" I couldn't imagine it. This clean-cut kid? "What were you accused of?" Okay, that wasn't the best English, but what do you say when your employee tells you that he was a felon?

"I was convicted of stealing an auto when I was eighteen," Cody said, blushing. "I wanted to see what it felt like being a thief."

"That's a silly reason to steal a car. And you were kind of old to go joy riding," I said.

Cody shrugged. "I was a stupid kid." And how old was he now? All of twenty-eight? "I had been playing video games — Grand Theft Auto. I wanted to try it for real."

"He did his time," Ted said, coming up. "He was on probation."

"And," I said to Detective Reed, "he was young. I trust my father to hire and keep honest people."

"I told him," Cody said.

"And he didn't put it into the file, because he didn't think it was important," I said. "If you hadn't told me just then, I never would have known it." I turned to Reed. "Case solved. Anything else?"

"We do have to consider him as a suspect."

I made a face. "Seems like a big jump from car theft to murder." I mused. "I got a parking ticket once. Are you going to charge me with murder?"

"Don't be ridiculous."

I sighed, suddenly tired of this man. "I didn't start it." I turned back to my fliers deliberately. "Is there anything else?" I would have loved to ask him how the case was going, but obviously, it wasn't going well, if they were down here, harassing my employees.

"You were seen at Hop-In talking about the case," Reed said.

"Of course," I said. "You didn't tell me not to."

"We would appreciate if you kept the details to yourself."

"And we would appreciate getting back to work," I said, a little bit louder than I expected. "Besides, I didn't share any details. I just asked about old Joe and what his background was."

"That's none..."

"That *is* my business, since he was discovered on my property."

"Still. I will ask you not to talk any more about the case. I can't force you. But I will warn you not to get in my way."

I blinked. "Or what?"

He stalked off. As soon as I heard the front door slam, I leaned back in my chair, then picked up my coffee.

My hands were shaking.

"You know," Ted said, "he's not that bad a man."

"I'm sure he's not. But he's pressing all of my buttons right now. I don't need that."

Cody came into my office. "Are you sure that that car incident won't bother you?"

I smiled. "We all do dumb things as teenagers."
Mind you, I thought, I had never stolen a car just to see
what it felt like, but I always knew that I would be drawn,
quartered, disowned, and other things by my parents if I
had ever done anything that dumb.

Cody smiled uncertainly and walked off. "Seems to
be a good kid," I said quietly to Ted.

Ted looked at Cody's retreating back. "Sometimes,"
he said slowly, "he seems to try *too* hard. I've seen him
have a bit of a temper."

"Oh?" I wouldn't have thought it. Not anybody who
looked like John Denver.

"But he's good with the customers."

"What's his story?"

"He moved in about four years ago. Came from a
small town in California, claimed he wanted to get back to
his roots here in the Midwest. His references were impecca-
ble, and he's had computer and bookkeeping training."

"Computer training?" I said. "But we don't have
computers."

"I think your Dad figured that we were going to get
them someday, so he had better start someone as support
for you."

I rolled my eyes. "You realize that if I hadn't been
out of work I wouldn't have moved back."

Ted smiled at me.

"You're not so sure?"

"I think that you might have run away, but this
place is in your bones." He nodded. "You would have
ended up back here, eventually."

"Still," I mused, "it would have easier had I been
born a boy."

"Well, yes," Ted agreed. "But the industry has to
change somewhere. You're not the only woman CEO."

I smiled at him. "You're rather progressive for your
age. So – when are you going to learn the computers?"

131

"I'm not that progressive," Ted grimaced.

"Then I'll guess we'll have to rely on Cody."

"Well, don't rely on me. I'm not touching the thing."

"I think you would be surprised on how easy it'll make your life -- here."

"I'm just going to leave it for Cody."

I looked at the computer again. "In fact, I wish I had one right now. It's amazing what one can find on the search engines."

"Like porn?" Ted grinned.

"Eeuw." I groaned. "I hadn't thought about that. Do I need to get child locks on it?"

"Well," Ted said, "I've heard of some awfully strange things happening around here."

"Yeah," I said quietly. "Like murder."

Ted sighed.

CHAPTER 12

I stood in the middle of my apartment and exhaled. It already seemed empty. I had lived here for the better part of fifteen years.

I suppose I should have felt sad, but the place was not filled with memories, happy or sad. It was just an apartment, neutral, waiting for the next occupants. I had thought to move to Detroit was to start over, to really live, to leave home.

But, even after fifteen years, I only had a few friends, none close, and some former co-workers.

I heard a knock on my door. I looked at it, wonderingly, then opened the door. A matronly woman stood there, smiling at me. I moved into her hug. "Barbara. How did you know I was here?"

It was my former co-worker and mentor. This was the one person I would miss in Detroit, yet I suspected I would miss her more than she would miss me. After all, she was retired and had children and grandchildren and a husband to keep her busy.

"I talked to your mother. She said you were here, packing up some of your stuff." A few tears came to her eyes. "Were you going to leave without saying goodbye?"

I could feel myself blushing. "Yes. No. I mean, I called, but I didn't get hold of you and when you didn't call back..."

"Oh, honey, I was at Amy's place, babysitting." Her daughter, Amy, lived in Boston, so that meant she was out of state. She had two daughters and a son. "I'm so sorry to hear about your father." She gave me another hug, then pushed me away. "And now you're moving out of town!" She looked sad.

"I'm sorry."

Barbara smiled. "No, you're not. I felt so bad when

I had to shut the company down. I could retire, but you were out of a job."

"I was doing all right."

"Your unemployment was about to run out."

"Well, yes." I smiled.

"And now you're the president of your own company!"

"My Mom's company," I said.

She shook her head. "Close enough." She held me by the shoulders. "Everything will be all right."

I chewed my lip. "Did Mom tell you what happened?"

Her face fell. "The murder. Yes." She looked ill. "Can I sit down?"

"Are you all right?" I said, concerned.

"I saw a murder once."

"Barbara!" In all of the years I knew her, she had never mentioned that.

"It was my first husband. He was stabbed in front of me."

"Oh. My. God." I had known that her first husband had passed, but I presumed that it had been a heart attack or an accident or something benign. "Murder?"

She nodded. Tears spilled down her cheeks. "We were out to dinner, and we were mugged. I'm sorry. It's been thirty years, but sometimes it feels like it was yesterday."

I hugged her. "I was going to ask you to visit sometime."

She wiped her tears. "Only if there's not going to be any more murders," she smiled. "I'm sorry to burden you like this, but I wanted to let you know that you're not alone."

"Oh, Barbara, I know I'm not alone."

"And I wanted to bring you this." She picked up her purse and pulled something out. It was a canister of pepper spray. "I always carry one with me now. I think you need to carry one with you."

"Or a good gun."

"No," she shook her head. "Less chance of being accused of murder with this."

"True." I sat for a minute. "Barbara, were you accused of your husband's murder?"

"Yes. For a time. I was the only witness."

"Did Mom tell you we were suspects?"

"Yes." She looked sharply at me. "Even if you aren't suspects, I'm pretty sure you're in danger. Your Mom doesn't think so, though."

"Neither do I." I thought of poor Joe. "Although I have to admit I can't figure out who would kill an addled little old man. A World War Two veteran."

"Perhaps if he had carried something like this..." Barbara held up the little canister.

"That's just it," I said. "From what I can see, he didn't try to defend himself."

"Maybe he was unconscious already."

"There was no sign of a stroke. Or a head wound. And his heart was beating when he was stabbed." Reed hadn't told me that; when I had looked into the hole, I had seen blood on his shirt.

I shivered.

Barbara was talking, and I put my mind back on the conversation. "Which meant that he knew his attacker, or thought he knew him."

"Or it could have been a woman." I thought of Ashley, then discounted that. If I started thinking that girl could murder people, then I'd be afraid of everybody in town.

"You're right," Barbara said. "My husband Ray's murderer was a teenager."

"A female?"

"No," Barbara said. "But he was just a little guy." She shook her head. "A little guy who had gotten hold of a

135

big knife and figured that we had some money."

"I'm sorry."

She stood up. "Well," she said, "I've scared you enough, but only because I'm worried for you."

I got up and gave her a big hug. "You know, people thought that I was asking for a mugging just living this close to Detroit."

Barbara grinned. "Really?"

I smiled sadly back. "So I move to the small town, where people keep their cars and their doors unlocked and someone gets murdered in my workplace."

"Sometimes life is a little too ironic," Barbara said. She pressed the pepper spray in my hands. "Keep this on you."

"I will."

"And I expect to come over some time. Just try to stop me."

"Wouldn't think of it. My Mom likes you."

"You going to find a place of your own?"

"Not right away."

"Good." Barbara nodded. "Your Mom needs some-one right now." She started moving toward the door. "Trust me. I know." She stopped again. "Oh, and don't necessarily trust the police."

I rolled my eyes. "Trust the police? Not a chance."

"Good," she smiled. We hugged again, and with a sad look, she left.

I sighed and looked around the apartment again. *Now* I was ready to leave.

<<<◇>>>

I collapsed into a chair at Mom's house — my house now, I corrected myself. Mom came out of the bed-room. "Honey," she said, "are you all right?"

"How in the world did Daddy handle it?" I said, dis-gusted.

"Tough day?"

"Three complaints, Sam didn't tighten down the tie-down straps so we had a whole load of two by fours on Main Street, and I had one customer and two salesmen ignore me and go directly to Ted because they figured he was the president."

"Well," Mom said calmly, "I never told you it was going to be easy. I will admit that if Daddy had had a chance to train you, it might have been easier on you. You would have had his blessing, so to speak."

"But I have your blessing."

"I'm just the wife," she said calmly and without bitterness.

"But if you hadn't been behind Daddy --"

"Then the business wouldn't have been successful as it was. Your father knew that and thanked me." She smiled. "Profusely."

"I never knew that."

"But we never let the town know."

I smiled.

Someone knocked on the door.

As if the day wasn't bad enough. "Detective Reed," I said, opening the door. "Don't you take any time off? Planning to accuse my mother while you're at it?"

"No." He had the grace to look abashed. "I just wanted to tell you that you are both officially off the suspect list."

"Really?" My voice dripped with irony.

"Carrie," Mom said. "Andy, will you come in?"

I stood at the door, looking at Reed, then reluctantly moved aside. "Will you have something to drink? Pop, water, coffee?"

"Oh, no, thank you," Reed said. "Actually, I was rather hoping you could help me."

"Us," Mom said, turning on the charm again, "help you?" She gestured toward a chair. "Won't you sit down?"

137

"I know you told me once," he said, sitting awkwardly at the edge of a chair, "but I wanted to double-check. Is there anyone around who wants to see the lumberyard closed down?" He waved away a glass of water. "I know about Mike Collingsworth."

"Why would you ask that?" She looked vaguely alarmed. "Is there someone else?"

"I heard a rumor today in the diner downtown that you were closing the yard. Now, I know you have no intention of closing the yard," he said, holding up his hand when Mom started to sputter indignantly, "but that's what's going around."

She chewed her lip. "I actually heard the same thing at church. Somebody came up to me and asked when we were closing down. She had heard that we were — quoting now — freaked out about the murder and that I couldn't bear to set foot in the place. She was very sympathetic with me about that." She turned to me. "By the way, I'm visiting you tomorrow. So don't be surprised when I come for a visit."

I grinned. "Should I clean the toilets and mop the floor?"

Mom smiled. "I'll wear my grungies." She turned to Reed. "But no, I hadn't heard of any other credible offers. The big chains keep talking about coming in, but I think this town is a little too small for them."

"Do you know anybody who would start such a rumor? A disgruntled employee? A disgruntled contractor?"

"There are always disgruntled contractors," Mom said.

I thought about the guy I had met when I first went there. "There's that Dick... Richard, I mean. Richard – um – Nathan."

Mom grinned. "He's not so bad. He talks rough, but he'll back down in a good fight."

I raised my eyebrows. "Sounds like you've tangled

138

with him."

"Had to, once. Your father had the flu once, and he had the nerve to call the house and complain about the quality of – oh, I don't remember what, now." She sat back in satisfaction.
"Not only did I ream him up and down for calling here, I convinced him that all of the yards carry the same quality of whatever it was. Shingles, I think. Common brand. He came around, especially after I threatened to have his account closed for harassing us at home."

Reed looked fascinated. "You didn't call the police?"

"Why?" Mom said. "It was just a little tiff. He didn't threaten anything, and the only thing I threatened was to cutoff his account." She smiled. "If the lumberyard called the police every time somebody yelled at them, the police would be down there once a day."

Reed relaxed. "I only worked in the hardware store for the little while. I'm used to being yelled at, but, after all, that comes with the job."

"So are we."

"It would probably help," I said, "if we had an idea why anybody would want to store him inside of barn three."

Reed looked at me sharply. "Who said he wasn't murdered in the barn?"

I closed my eyes. "In spite of what you might think, I do have eyes."

He looked puzzled.

"No blood splatter. I may not have police education, but I do watch CSI."

He groaned and lowered his head into his hands. "Lord save me from amateurs." He lifted his head. "I don't suppose I could deny it."

"Not exactly," Mom said. "I should tell you that she notices everything."

"Except what I don't want to notice."

"I can tell."

CHAPTER 13

A month later, not much had happened with the case, and it was the day before Thanksgiving and inventory time. I had never actually been involved in an inventory before; I had adjusted inventory for clients, but as far as the physical inventory – no. I looked out into the yard at the swirling snow. "Wonderful," I muttered.

"It has to be done once a year," Ted chuckled. And we've been doing inventory the day after Thanksgiving since before your father owned this place."

"I know, I know," I muttered. "Good thing I have a snowsuit, isn't it?"

"Well, if it's any consolation," Ted said, "we do the inside first."

I looked at the guys already counting. "Small consolation. Looks like they'll have it mostly done before tomorrow."

"You'll be surprised."

"Is there anything we can do outside?"

"Well," Ted said, "we can go out to the back and make sure things are straightened up."

I sighed. "Well, it will beat staying in here and watching people count." I could do that; I had already written all the invoices I could and I couldn't do any posting until the day was done. I was restless. "I'll get my winter coat on." I wasn't sure how much a woman and an almost retired man could move, but it was better than sitting in here, waiting for the phone to ring late on the afternoon before Thanksgiving.

Of course, I could take off and do some pre-Black Friday shopping, but that seemed a bit chicken, especially since I was supposed to be president.

I *was* president.

I still had a hard time believing it.

I was still having a hard time believing my Daddy was gone. In my mind, he was still the president and I was just the temporary caretaker. My logical part told me that he was gone, and I had better get used to this, but my emotional mind still couldn't believe it.

I sighed, got my coat, and waited for Ted.

"Where to first?"

"How about number seven?"

Number seven was an open shed in the back where we stored our treated wood. "Sounds good to me."

We exited the office, went across the railroad tracks, and passed barn number three. Involuntarily, I glanced at the opening where Joe was found, then walked fast past it. Ted looked at me, then caught up with me. "Ted, I don't think I can ever look at that building the same way again."

Ted nodded. "You won't. I should know." He didn't elaborate any further, nor did I force him. I learned that from my Dad.

It took only a minute to reach the back fence. I glanced at the piles. "That's... a mess."

"I figured we could at least pick up and straighten up the smaller boards. Makes it easier to count."

I looked at the four by four by sixteens. "I hope you weren't talking about those."

"Hardly."

"Shouldn't the guys be doing this?" I said, while we were moving boards. "After all, this isn't exactly in our worker's comp."

Ted chuckled. "Well, generally, the guys do this, but you looked like you were about ready to jump out of your skin in there. I figured a little physical activity wouldn't hurt."

As we lifted boards, I had to admit he was right. As I lifted the last board, I stopped and stared, then turned away and started to gag.

"What is it?" Ted said, alarmed.

I pointed. He looked. "Oh."

There, behind the last boards – I can hardly bear to think of it – were some tiny little bodies. Cats, and raccoons, and one or two of animals I couldn't recognize right away. All of them were mutilated in some way. The last few looked like they had their throats cut.

"Oh, my God," I finally said when I could breathe. "Oh, my God."

"That would explain why I haven't seen many cats lately," Ted said, speculatively.

"That's horrible."

"I agree." He seemed calm, but I looked at him. He appeared to be as sickened as I was.

"Why would anybody do that?"

"There are," Ted said, looking at the animals, "a lot of sick people out there. The question is who would do this, and why back here?"

True. I looked around. "We have a closed yard."

"Which means that anybody would have to do this during the day." Ted looked around, speculatively.

"Either that, or we have another hole in the fence."

We followed the fence. "There it is." I sighed. "Somebody else is getting in. And I just got the insurance check for the other one."

"We need to call Stetson."

"Why?" Okay, that sounded petulant, even to me.

"Don't you think this might be connected to the murder?"

I stared at him. "I hadn't thought quite that far."

"Let's go back into the office."

"Why?" I said. I pulled out my cell. "I think I'd rather not let the rest of the office know until I get his interpretation."

"You're going to call Stetson?" Ted said. "After all your arguing?"

"Well," I said, "for one thing, this two-bit town" (I smiled to take out the sting) "only has one detective. And, if we hadn't had a murder here, I wouldn't have bothered." I looked Ted in the eye. "I can't help but think that they're all connected."

Ted looked at the disgusting pile. "You're probably right." He looked again. "What I can't understand is why this pile didn't smell before this. Some of these bodies are obviously old."

"Unless they were just placed."

"In which case, this would be a warning."

Ted blinked. "But then, how would they know that we two were cleaning up boards this afternoon?"

"Probably just lucky chance. Someone knew we were doing inventory Friday and knew these were going to be found."

"Okay," I said. "I'm calling." I waited for the phone to ring, and it started snowing harder. "Detective Reed, this is Carrie Burton."

"I know," he sounded amused. "I could tell by your caller ID."

Why did he do that?

144

"We have something we need to show you here in the lumber yard." My voice started shaking.

Suddenly, he was all business. "What? Are you all right?"

"I'm... fine." I said. "Come through the yard to the back. Ted and I will be waiting."

Ted was already on the walkie-talkie, telling Jimmy not to get excited, but Detective Reed was coming back to the back of the yard. He deflected any questions.

It wasn't five minutes before Reed pulled back beside us. He jumped out of the car. "What is it?" He looked at my face. "Are you sure you're all right?"

I pointed behind the pile of treated boards. He peered over, then started back. He looked at me, then at the animals. "Oh." He said.

"We've decided that since nobody smelled anything back here, that this must have been just dumped," Ted said.

"Which puts another whole meaning to the word disturbing and creepy," I muttered. Who would want to move a bunch of dead animal bodies? Just for a warning? Eeuw. Murdering the poor things was bad enough.

"We'll need," said Reed, looking pale himself, "to take these for evidence." He looked revolted at the task.

"Is there anybody around that can help?"

"I think in this case, I may – recruit some people. Like Dr. Thompson." Dr. Thompson was our local veterinarian. Nice man, he had been into the yard a few times. I'm sure he would hate to do this, but I wasn't sure our local coroner was up to this.

"And we'll get a couple of policemen to

help," he added.

He turned to us. "I know this seems like an odd question, but I have to ask it. Have you seen anybody suspicious around here lately?"

"Not really, not since the funeral," I said."

"Vince?"

"I nodded. "I see him around town every weekend."

"I thought I had seen him, too," Reed muttered. "Has he been bothering you?"

"Just being in the same town as he is bothers me," I said that a little sharper than I had intended. "But no," I added, softening my tone. "I wish I could put a protection order against him, but there's nothing illegal in being annoying."

"Sadly, true," Reed said. "What about Mike Collingsworth? I seem to remember that he said something about making you uncomfortable."

"He's another one that does it by his presence," I said. "He comes up to Mom every couple of weeks asking whether she's reconsidering selling; usually, she's out eating at the time." I smiled wanly. "Mom swears that one of these days, she's going to accidentally upend a soup on his head."

Reed chuckled. "I'm going to pretend I didn't hear that so that when it happens, I can be properly shocked."

I grinned back, momentarily forgetting about the pitiful little bodies behind the boards.

"What kind of person would kill animals for a warning?" Ted asked.

Boom. That brought me straight back to earth.

"Someone who doesn't value any life whatsoever, except where it could benefit them."

I shivered.

146

"I hope that's not what we're dealing with," he said.

"These are," I said, "our yard cats. I had wondered what had happened to them. I had just gotten them to approach people." I started crying. "I never should have tried."

Reed came up to me and pulled me toward him. I ended up crying into his chest. "I'm sorry," I cried.

Reed patted me on the back. "You're all right." He said. "Anybody would be shook up by this."

Gradually, in the back of my mind, I noticed how broad his chest was. He was comfortable. There was no other word to describe it.

I pushed back. I didn't want to be comfortable in Detective Stetson Reed's arms. I didn't even like Reed.

Sure I didn't.

"I had better let you get to work," I said.

He cleared his throat. "I'll start to make some phone calls."

It didn't take long for the regular police to show up. Three cars came in; I would have liked to see the reaction of the guys in the office to the one car that came in with his lights on. I glanced at Reed. "For animals? Really?"

He blushed slightly. "Adam's new. I'll talk to him."

Just then, I noticed a movement out of the corner of my eye.

One of the cats was moving.

It was a kitten. I hadn't noticed it before, because I hadn't wanted to look. Why it hadn't moved before, I don't know, but it was moving now. It nudged against an older one. I presume it was the mother – I hadn't had a chance to get acquainted with the resident cat population too much yet. It pushed at her with its head, then started wailing.

"Oh, no," Reed said. He climbed over the pile of boards and picked the kitten up, holding it to his chest. It was a calico. He cuddled it, petting it, trying to keep it from being so frantic. Finally, it butted its head, hiding its eyes.

I moved forward, petting the poor thing's back. Reed looked at me. "Let me take it," I whispered.

"It's probably evidence," he said. "I should process it."

"I think you have enough evidence," I said sharply. "Don't you?"

He looked at the kitten's bottom. "Still, we should probably have the vet look at her."

I blinked. "You can sex cats?"

He shrugged. "We had cats when I was a kid."

"So did we. But..."

He handed the kitten to me. "I should work."

I put her inside my coat. She clung on and buried her face again. Gradually, I could feel her relax, then I heard a tiny purr.

The police looked over the pile. "Yuch," said one.

Somehow, I never imagined police before saying yuch.

Reed turned to us. "Do you think," I said, "that this has anything to do with the murder?"

He shook his head. "I can't say that yet. It could be a warning; it could be something unrelated..." He looked slightly lost. "Unless I find a note or something, I won't know."

The kitten dug her tiny claws into my chest.

"Well, I said, I think I'm going to take Josie inside."

"What about the vet?"

"Can you send him inside when you're done?"

We walked back into the office. "What's going on out there?" Jimmy asked. Cody just looked at us wide-eyed.

"We found..." I couldn't continue. I went back to my office and cuddled the kitten. It kneaded my chest for a long time, then went to sleep on my desk. I stared out the window, then decided that if I continued to think about what was happening at Barn Number six over and over, I had to work to get my mind off of it. Really, I wanted to get out of there, but I didn't want to give Detective Reed a heart attack by taking off.

Ted came back. "I told them."

"How did they react?"

He sat down. "Shocked. Matthew was mad."

I raised my eyebrows. "I don't believe I've ever seen Matthew mad."

"I have. Always when innocents are involved."

"And what about Sam?"

Ted sighed. "You know him. No reaction."

"I know he's a good yard manager," I said. "But does he have some hidden qualities that I don't know about?"

"Like I said. It's just you he doesn't like."

"Gee, thanks," I said. I had a thought. "He wouldn't have done anything like that, would he?"

"Since he's adopted three dogs and two cats, no, I doubt it." Ted said dryly.

"Who would do something like this?" I got up and paced the office. The kitten purred and laid her head down. "It has to be a warning. Otherwise, why not just dump the corpses in the river? And most of those were lumberyard cats. Including Josie here."

"Josie?"

"Seems to fit." I shrugged.

"We have to consider that it may be just a sick mind," Ted said.

"Vince."

"Do you think he's capable of something like that?"

I thought a second. "No. At least, I don't think so. He's creepy enough without doing something like that."

"Mike Collingsworth."

I paced the office again. "You know him better than I do. He's another creepy looking guy, but I'm not sure that he would do something like that."

"No." Ted said decisively. "He wouldn't."

"Is there anybody else we would know?"

"I wouldn't think so."

"I'd like to see the tear in the fence. Was it from the outside in, or the inside out?"

"It looked like it was cut from the outside, going in," Ted said. "But, Carrie, that doesn't mean anything."

"True."

"Are you thinking that one of the employees did this?" Ted asked.

"Present company excepted," I said. "Quite frankly, you're the only one I know that well."

"I could have flipped," Ted said with a grin. "I could have caved under the pressure."

I grinned back. "And I could have caved under the pressure of my father dying and a harmless old man being murdered in my lumberyard, and I could have started torturing cats and stray animals for my jollies. So let's not be ridiculous." My smile faded.

"But Carrie," Ted said, looking at me earnestly, "that's the way I feel about everybody here. I'll admit that I don't know Cody as well as the others, and Sam has his funny moments."

"Funny?"

"I shouldn't have said that." Ted said. "I'm sorry. I wanted you to get to know him better."

"What?"

"About three years ago, Sam had a bad concussion. For a while there, they thought they were going to lose him. He pulled through, but his personality was changed. He seems more suspicious than he ever was. He used to joke, now we can't pull a joke out of him. And, very occasionally, I've caught him staring out into space with a blank look on his face." Ted shook his head.

"The misogyny?"

Ted picked up a pencil and started playing with it. "Oh," he said. "That's always been there to a certain extent. That hasn't changed."

I saw Detective Reed coming down the aisle, followed by Dr. Thompson. "You're all cleared."

"Did you find anything?"

He sighed. "No. But if you find anything, let me know."

The doctor stepped forward. "This is the kitten?"

"Yes."

He picked her up, gently. The kitten woke up immediately and looked him in the face. She then licked one of his fingers. "Well, hello to you too, sweetie." He felt the kitten all over, then looked her in the eye. "She seems to be fine. I'll take her with me." He looked at me questioningly. "Should I try to find someone to adopt her?"

"No," I said, hoping fervently that Mom wouldn't kill me for this. "I'll take Josie."

"Josie, hmm?" He looked at her again. "She looks to be around eight to ten weeks. Have you had a cat before?"

I nodded, remembering the late, great, black Zen cat that passed away a couple of years ago. "But I've never had a kitten this young."

"I'll give you some suggestions. In the meantime, can I keep her overnight for observation? And I'll get her started on her first shots."

"I'm planning to keep her indoors."

The Doctor nodded. "Okay."

I took the kitten back for a second. "Now, Josie," I said, "you go with this nice Doctor and I'll see you tomorrow."

She stared me in the face and licked my finger and started buzzing again.

"Right," I said. "We're agreed."

I caught Ted and Reed grinning at me. "So." I said.

"Nothing."

I watched the vet take Josie, then I returned back to the office. "We're taking inventory on Friday. Is there anything we should keep watch for?"

Reed frowned. "You should be all right," he said. "If you see anything suspicious, let me know, but otherwise...."

He looked us, then chewed his lip.

"What?"

"I just can't understand it. What's been stirred up in this place all of a sudden? I don't like it."

"Nobody here likes it," I said, a little sharper than intended.

"I keep expecting another shoe to drop," he said. "I just hope that it won't."

"We have a murder of an old man and an animal massacre. I've never heard of anything like this happening here."

"Almost sounds Pagan," Ted said.

"Oh, no," I said. "Not Pagan."

Ted looked at me questioningly.

"I have some good friends who are Pagan. I also have some Wiccan friends. None of them would even think of doing something like this."

"Really," Reed said.

"Of course, they wouldn't." I turned on him angrily.

Reed held up his hands. "No, no, I'm sorry. That's not what I meant. I was just surprised that you have Pagan and Wiccan friends. I didn't phrase that very well."

"No," I said, still annoyed. "You didn't. Just because I'm a Christian doesn't mean..."

"I know."

Ted looked at Reed. "You know, I think you had better find an exit line here."

"'See you next week' sounds good right now," Reed said.

"Right," I said. I turned away from him and looked at the window.

Why were these things happening?

CHAPTER 14

Mom pulled the chicken out of the oven while I stirred up the stuffing. "I want your promise," she said. "that there will be no murder talk at the table."

Well. That came out of left field. "I wasn't planning on it," I said. "Were you?"

"I invited a friend for dinner."

And yet another jagged turn.

"Oh?"

"He should be getting here right about now."

As if by clockwork, the front doorbell rang. My mind had already made the jump from murder and our houseguest, so I wasn't surprised to see Detective Reed on her doorstep.

"I was told," I said, without preamble, "that we weren't supposed to talk about murder."

Reed raised his eyebrows. "I wasn't planning on it. It's Thanksgiving." He paused. "Unless you're talking about killing the turkey."

I smiled. "Funny. Funny."

"I have my moments," he said, "even if you don't believe me."

"I haven't seen many funny moments yet," I said.

"Carrie," Mom called. "Are you going to invite him in?"

I blushed. "I'm sorry," I said. "Won't you come in?"

"Mothers," he murmured. "Can't live with 'em, can't live without 'em."

"Yeah," I smiled, then looked at him. "I thought your..." Then I kicked myself.

"Dead, yes," his eyes went bleak. "But I had

an aunt who pretty much adopted me after that. And three other aunts I visited."

"Really," I said.

"So for a long time, I had multiple mothers."

"Ah." I remembered my manners again. "Let me take your coat and get you something to drink. Water? Cola? Wine?"

"I have to be on duty later," he said, "so I'll take a cola."

"Then please sit down." I went into the kitchen and got a glass. "Mother," I whispered. "How could you?"

"How could I what?" Mom said, serenely. "And don't whisper. Most detectives have extremely fine hearing."

"I'm surprised you invited him without telling me?"

She shrugged. "I thought you might object."

I winced. "I wouldn't object, I guess, so much, but I might question the wisdom."

"He's good looking, isn't he?" she whispered.

"Sure," I whispered back. "Now you whisper." I grabbed his Coke and took it to the detective.

He was good looking, I had to admit that. I looked at his blue, blue eyes, and almost forgot to speak. In spite of myself, I looked at him surreptitiously. He was my kind of handsome. His black hair was tousled. He had a strong dimpled chin. His cheekbones were high, in an Italian sort of way. His shoulders were broad, and what I could see of his chest – which wasn't much – was chiseled. This policeman didn't sit around in cars and eat doughnuts.

I realized I had forgotten to speak. "I'm sorry, what did you say?"

"I was wondering if you heard how Josie

156

was."

Yes. The kitten. "I decided, since we didn't have any cat things here yet, that the best place for her was the vet."

Mom walked in. "I'm actually looking forward to having a cat here for a while."

For a while?

"I'm glad," Reed said. "I've always had a fond spot for cats, but I've never had one."

"Why not?"

He shrugged. "I guess I figured I had too much time at work."

"You do seem to be working all of the time." I said. "Do you ever get any time off?"

"Today."

"And we are glad." Mom went up to him and laid a hand on his arm.

"Why didn't you go to your aunts' house?"

"They're in Florida."

"Already?" Mom said. "John and I talked about it..." She looked sad. "Well, anyway, we wouldn't have gone this early in the season." A buzzer went off in the kitchen. "Andy, will you help me get the bird out?"

"Of course, Marie." He got up quickly, leaving me to follow them both. I happened to glance down – Detective Reed had a nice...

Uh-huh. Still, I wondered that I hadn't notice that part of his anatomy before. Too busy being annoyed by him, I guess.

He got the turkey out and carved it, under Mom's instruction. Everything else was ready, so we sat down at the table and Mom said Grace. After we all admired Mom's cooking – she was a good cook, even though she denied it – Reed turned to me. "So. I understand that you write fantasy."

157

I turned to Mom. "He wondered what you did for fun," she shrugged.

"I do," I said. "But it's just for my own entertainment."

Reed shrugged. "If you ever want to share, I'll look at it."

I blinked. "You read fantasy?"

"And Science Fiction. And media tie-ins..." he said, and we had an interesting talk about fiction, fan fiction, and other Geeky things, while Mom smiled indulgently and served Thanksgiving dinner.

As the conversation wore down, I looked at him. "I'm surprised, Detective Reed."

"By what?"

"Don't take this the wrong way, but usually someone as – _ " I just about said good-looking, but caught myself in time – "normal looking as you are doesn't read fantasy."

"I – um – might say the same thing as you?"

"Oh. Well. I was a geeky-looking child who didn't relate to a lot of my classmates. Science Fiction and fantasy was my retreat."

"And she was, too," Mom contributed. "I can show you pictures."

Thanks, Mom.

"It was pretty much the same thing with me." He hesitated. "You ever see Disney's Hercules?"

"Yeah?"

"I was the before pictures." He sighed. "After my parents were... gone... I applied myself to a lot of self-improvement. But I never lost my love for fiction."

"Interesting."

"Fascinating, I might say." We sat in silence for a second.

"Do you read any of your daughter's fiction, Marie?"

Mom actually shivered. "Um. No. Give me a good cozy mystery. My tastes run more to Hercule Poirot, Miss Marple, and Brother Cadfael." She sighed. "I just wish we could solve this local mystery." She looked at me. "I know, I know, I'm not going to talk about it."

We had some pumpkin pie, then went into the living room. "Well," Reed said, "I should go. I have to start work in an hour, and I need to get home and change."

"So soon?" Mom said.

I went to grab his coat out of the closet. "Well, Detective," I said, "it was a pleasure to have you here."

"Thank you for inviting me." He opened the door, then just as quickly closed it. He turned with his back to the door. "You don't want to go out there."

But I had caught a glimpse. There was a line of rabbits with their throats slit on our porch. At the end of the line was a Barbie doll, with a red line across its throat.

This message couldn't have been clearer.

<<<<>>>>

The vet had been there – again – and taken the sad little corpses off of our porch. We sat with Reed in the living room. "I'm not sure I want to stay here overnight," I said, looking at Mom.

"If it helps," Reed said, "I have a volunteer to watch your house overnight."

"That *would* make me feel better," Mom said. "But I guess I don't understand why they're targeting us."

"They want to drive us out of town," I said.

159

"Yes," Mom said ironically. "I gathered that. But why not attack us directly? Why are they torturing animals? Why not shoot at the house or break in or beat us up?"

"I really didn't need to have that in my imagination." I shivered.

"I'm not sure," Reed said slowly, "that we're dealing with an entirely sane individual here. Because I have to say that I agree."

"Do you think that Joe's murder and the murder of these little animals are connected?"

"My logical mind would like to say no," Reed said.

"That's what I think, too." I sighed. "But how did he know that Ted and I were going to clean up the treated boards?"

"I'm sure he didn't," Reed said. "That was just a happy coincidence for him."

"Wonderful," I said. "Well, I know who my major suspects are."

"Who?" Mom said.

"Well, Vince, for one." I said. "He doesn't think I can do anything without him. He's probably expecting me to come screaming for male protection from the boogieman."

"But you are getting male protection," Reed said.

"But not from him," I countered. "If I thought I could actually hit something, I would sit on the front porch with a shotgun, like one of those stereotypical old hillbillies."

"Thank you for not doing that," Mom said ironically. "But I would join you, if it came to that."

"Have you seen Vince lately?" Reed said.

"Well, no," I admitted. "But that doesn't mean anything."

"And your other suspect," Mom said.

"Mike Collingsworth."

"The man who wants to buy the yard." Mom sighed. "I do have to admit that these tactics are scaring me a bit."

"Yeah," I said. "Me, too. But I don't want to sell the yard, and I certainly don't want to run away like a rat on a sinking ship."

Mom grinned.

"Bad analogy."

"Do you want to delay inventory tomorrow?" she asked.

"No." I said. "But I do have admit I'd feel better about it if you weren't home alone tomorrow. Do you want to sit in?"

"I might even work."

I smiled at her.

"Well, after all, I can count to greater than ten."

"Never doubted you could," I said.

Reed grinned uncertainly.

CHAPTER 15

We made it through inventory in record time, even though Mom and I were looking over our shoulders. In the middle of the afternoon, both of us were looking for a hot chocolate, and we settled on McDonald's best.

This McDonald's had a bit of a fishing theme to go along with all of the lakes around the county. There were pictures of trout and sunfish and bluegill and even the occasional catfish. Different kinds of fishing poles were stuck up on the walls, and there was a case full of different kinds of tackle and artificial bait.

I used to fish with Dad, many years ago, but hadn't been out since I was a teenager. But the place brought back good memories for me.

We picked a booth looking toward the downtown area. As we sat there, waiting to warm up, Reed found us. "How did it go?" he said, standing over the table.

"Oh, fine." Mom said. "No other nasty surprises, except for the nasty bunch of two by fours in the middle of an otherwise good bunk."

Reed looked puzzled.

"It's a retail thing," I said. "Anyway, we have the rest of the weekend off."

"You should go away," he suggested. "I don't think anyone would think it chicken of you if you went to a hotel."

"But... what if they target the house?"

"You know," Reed said, looking at the distance, "they haven't targeted things yet, just animals. And Joe. And besides, if they do target your house, number one," he pointed up a finger, "I have it under observation, and two, I'd rather you not be in it if it was targeted."

"We'll find something in Kalamazoo," Mom said, immediately. "Besides, it'll be fun. I've been wanting to get to a pool."

"I don't know," I said. "It still feels like running away. If it's Vince, I want to confront him, if it's someone else... I guess I'd worry more in Kalamazoo than if I stayed here."

"I can't force you to do what you don't want to do," Reed looked at me intensely. "But I would feel better if you were away from the house and the lumberyard."

"But you can't force us away," I said, my stubbornness rearing its head.

"Carrie?" Mom said. "I can stay in the house. Why don't you go away?"

"And leave you alone? No way."

Mom turned to Reed. "I guess we're staying, Andy."

He glared at me. I glared back.

"Why don't you sit down and have a coffee, Andy," Mom said, looking at the two of us.

"Oh, no, thank you, Marie. I need to get back to work."

"A shame," Marie said. "But we all have to do it, I guess."

He smiled at her. "That's the way it goes." He bought a coffee and left the restaurant.

Mom turned to me. "Carrie, your stubbornness may be the death of me."

I rolled my eyes. "But Mom, I meant what I said. I am not going to run away from this. If I do that, I might as well give up any real idea of being president. Can you imagine what that would look like to the employees?"

164

"Jimmy and Ted would think that you were being smart," Mom said.

I sighed. "Yes, but they knew me when I was in pigtails."

Mom smiled. "Carrie, you were never in pigtails."

"Figuratively, Mom."

"But Cody and Mathew and Sam only knew me as an adult. I feel that I can admit ignorance in front of them, but I can't admit cowardice."

"I don't think you're giving them enough credit," Mom said. "But I have to admit that I don't know them that well."

"I'm getting to know them," I said, letting myself get distracted. "Cody seems to be enthusiastic and has a lot of energy. Mathew is calming — I think when Ted retires, we should bring him into the office. I believe he'll make a good salesman, and certainly he can use the money."

"And Sam?" Mom prompted.

"And Sam," I sighed. "I can't seem to get to know him. He obeys my orders and Ted's orders, but he just seems to keep to himself."

"Sam," Mom said, looking out the window and lifting her coffee. She took a sip, then continued. "Sam is an odd one. Your father told me once that he had a tragic background, but he wouldn't tell me what it was."

"Apparently, nothing too bad, or Reed would have found it." I took a sip of coffee myself and kept my hands around the cup. They were still cold. "Did I tell you that Reed came in, claiming that Cody had a record?"

"Cody?" Mom said.

"Said that he had stolen a car. Cody said it was a mistake, so I defended him."

"I sometimes wonder about Cody," Mom said.

"Really?"

"Who moves to Southern Michigan from Southern California—Los Angeles, in fact," she said, putting her cup down. "Without family here or friends? And gets a job in a small lumberyard out in the middle of nowhere?" She looked at the tackle on the wall. "Your father didn't think it was odd, but I always did. I always wondered if he didn't have something to hide."

I shrugged. "I'm sure if he did, Reed would have found it."

"Only if something was recorded."

I looked at my Mom. "And you claim I have a nasty imagination?"

"Not imagination, dear," she said, looking troubled. "Intuition. But my intuition has been known to be wrong," she smiled, and the troubled look vanished. "Maybe he just wanted to get away from a bad relationship or a bad family—or who knows? Still..."

I laughed. "You're making him sound like Vince. I'm sure he's nothing like Vince. Dad or Ted would have discovered something in all of this time."

Mom took another sip of coffee. "Want to blow your diet and eat here?"

"You're evading the point."

"Yes," Mom said. "Yes, I am."

"Yes," I said. "I'll take a Big Mac."

<<<<>>>>

Friday night was peaceful, so I decided to keep the appointment I already had for the next day. I couldn't stand it any longer, I had to get rid of the large skunk line I had in the part of my hair. But the last hairdresser I had gone to in Herculaneum had passed away two years before, so Mom gave me her recommendation.

After fussing back about the proper color, Joni started applying the color. The shop was a small place, with an open showroom like front, so I could see everybody pass by and they could see me. In the midst of the color, I sat bolt upright, almost leaving behind a hank of hair in her hand.

"What!" Joni said. "Did I hurt you?"

I stared out the window. "Damn," I said. "I thought maybe he had given up."

She looked out the window. "Who?"

"Vince."

"Vince?" She started working on my hair again. "I'm sorry, honey, I'm not following you."

"Ex-boyfriend. Stalker."

"Oh," she said. "Say no more."

"Look," I said, and turned the chair around to slip out Reed's card. "Could you be casual and call Detective Reed at the phone number I'm going to give you?"

"Honey, I can be as casual as you want."

She did my hair a little more, then moved to the phone as if she were answering it, even saying "Hello?" to the dial tone. Casually, she hid the phone from the window, then dialed the number. "Andy?" she said. "Carrie Burton wanted me to call you. Her ex-boyfriend is looking at her from across the street—right. I'll tell her." She acted as if she was writing down an appointment in her book, then said goodbye and hung up the phone. "He'll be right over."

"Good." I told her what had been going on. "I don't know if he killed all of those poor animals, but he shouldn't be following me around, either."

"If he makes a move toward this shop, I'll get him with my Karate." I looked up at her. She was completely serious. "Brown belt."

"I didn't think you were supposed be aggressive with Karate."

"Aggressive, hell. When it comes to protection of my customers..." She did a pose toward the mirror, and I broke out laughing, "I'm going to be as aggressive as hell."

"Maybe I should have you follow me around," I was saying, when Reed walked in.

"Hi, Joni," he said.

"Hi, Andy," she responded. "The creep was sitting over there in front of Jamesson's bookstore, staring right in the window."

He glanced out the window. "He's moving down the street."

With a swift move, he was out the door, then I saw him confront Vince. Vince started arguing, then punched Reed. Joni gasped, and my mouth dropped open. "Oh," Joni said. "That was a mistake."

In a moment, Reed had knocked Vince down, had his hands behind his back, and had him cuffed.

"I'm brown belt," Joni said, admiringly, "but Andy is the top black belt in my dojo."

"I think," I said, "I should learn some Karate."

We finished the rest of the appointment. I kept grinning, thinking of Vince in jail.

The rest of the weekend went well. If our house was being watched, even I couldn't see where they were watching from. My heart rose with every passing hour, and I was in a good mood when I went to work on Monday morning.

Until I unlocked the front door.

At seven in the morning in Michigan in late November, the sun hasn't risen yet. When I pulled in, I looked up at the streetlight. It was out. I hadn't noticed it was out before; it must have burned out over the weekend. I parked the car in the yard and crossed the railroad tracks, opened up the back door. A couple of minutes later, Cody and Mathew drove in, followed by Jimmy and Sam. Ted was last, and he looked a little haggard—must be his wife had a bad night. As soon as seven rolled around, I unlocked the front door, opened it to make sure everything was all right, and shrieked at what the light showed.

Nailed to the front door was a raccoon, spread-eagled.

Thank God, he was dead.

"What the hell," Ted said. He started swearing under his breath. "I'm calling the police."

"Go for it," I said, going back into the main office and sitting down. The only thing I could think of was that it couldn't be Vince, Reed had him locked up through this morning on resisting arrest and causing harm to a public officer. Then who could it be?

My mind went in circles. Was it Richard Nathan? If so, why hadn't he said more? Shouldn't threats be matched with demands of some sort or another?

Was it some sicko who had targeted me for some reason? Like saying that ladies couldn't run lumber yards? If so, why torture animals and show them off at me? I like animals as well as the next girl, but I wasn't exactly associated with animals, I thought. Was that just coincidence?

What in the devil was going on here?

CHAPTER 16

So when I saw the letter tacked up next to the poor animal, it was almost a relief. I lifted up the letter gingerly into the light, using a tissue. It was so stereotypical, the letter was almost funny. In fact, if I didn't know better, I would have accused one of my old roommates of writing it.

It was made of newspaper headlines. "Them animals was just warnings," it read. "Get out of town while you still can."

The guy must have spent hours getting high on glue just to do this little message!

Cody ripped it from the tack violently. "Cody! The police need that for evidence," I said.

"We don't need that on the front door," he muttered.

I took it from him with the tissue and carried it into to the main office, then spread it out on the counter and looked at it. Like all of the stereotypical notes, it seemed to be made out of a combination of newspaper, slick paper, and magazine ads. I studied it over carefully, but I couldn't get anything more out of it than the average layperson. I sighed. Jimmy got up and looked at the letter. "You need to call Detective Reed, Carrie."

"I know, I know. It just seems like I've been calling him every two minutes." I looked at it again. "I just wanted to see if I could figure something out before I called him."

Cody walked up. "I called the police." He looked down at the letter. "You know," he said, "leaving town is probably not a bad idea."

I snorted. "Have you been talking to Reed?"

Cody thinned his lips. "He accused me of auto theft. Next time he comes around, I swear I'm going to hit him."

I smiled at him, but my smile faded. It looked like he was completely serious. "Please. Don't. None of us need the trouble that would cause."

"He had better not accuse me of anything again, then."

I smiled. "I'm sure he won't."

Sam had come into the office from the back, blowing into his hands. "It's as cold as a—" He stopped short. "Sorry, ma'am."

"Cold as a bitch, huh?" I smiled at him. "Sam, I'm not a shrinking violet."

"Don't seem right to swear in front of a lady," he muttered.

My eyebrows rose. Everybody was acting atypical today. "I'm not a lady," I said. "I'm female, but I ain't necessarily a lady."

In spite of himself, the corners of his mouth came up. "You always seemed like one."

I shrugged. "I worked in an office where I had to learn to be a lady." I looked at him. "Dad never let me come down here much when I was a kid, and when I *was* old enough to work down here, I refused."

"Yeah. I didn't want to work in my father's business, either." Sam looked almost surprised that he said that, but he went on. "Then again, my father was a prison guard."

I blinked. "Really?"

"Yeah."

"I may ask you for story ideas later."

Sam looked at me oddly.

"My hobby is writing stories."

"Oh. Never put much stock in books and stuff."

This was the most open conversation I had had with Sam. Too bad it was in front of everybody else—then it struck me. I was trying to go about talking to these guys as ladies talk to each other. I had little experience talking to guys as—well—guys.

"That's okay," I finally answered. "I don't watch

football games." I knew Sam was a fan of the Lions; I had overheard them talk football at break time.

Ted walked in from the front door, looking grim. He caught Sam smiling at me and cocked an eyebrow. "Ted!" I said, turning serious. "I need you to look at this."

He glanced at it, then lifted up the phone and handed it to me. "Call Reed. Now."

"Cody called the police."

"You should call Reed, too," Ted said grimly.

I thought about saying "Do I have to?" but I restrained myself. Cody turned away. Jimmy sat down. "Reed. Carrie Burton. I have something here you need to see."

"What is it?" came his voice, rather tinny. It sounded as if it were underwater. Cell service isn't good in this area."

"I'd rather show you. Look at the front door when you come."

"I'll be right there." And that was literal. Two minutes later, he was pulling up out front. He paused at the front door. Behind him came the police. I could almost see the police lady look and say, "Oh, that's just wrong." They talked a minute, then Reed walked in while the police lady went to the car, got some evidence bags and gloves. I could see the look of distaste through the glass of the door, but she was efficient and quick.

Thank heavens.

Reed looked at the counter. "What else do you have?"

I pointed to the letter on the counter. "I used a tissue."

Reed winced.

"I don't buy the tissues with the lotion built in."

"Good." He pulled out gloves and picked it up. "I'll take this with me, if you don't mind."

"Cody ripped it off of the tack," I said. "So it might

have his fingerprints on it."

"Yeah?" He looked at Cody. "I'll need your prints to eliminate you."

Cody smiled. "Gladly."

He pulled a kit out of his pocket. "Do you have a TARDIS in your pocket?"

"Naw, just Mary Poppin's carpetbag." He smiled, and the rest of the crew looked blank. "I thought I might need the fingerprint kit. I carry it in my car."

"Really?"

I watched as he took Cody's fingerprints.

Mom walked in, looked at Reed just putting the kit away, and looked at me. "Trouble?"

"Why would there be trouble?" I said innocently.

Mom looked exasperated.

"I got a threatening letter," I said, dismissively.

"As if the dead animals weren't enough?" Mom said.

I must have looked pale. She looked around. "Let's go back to the office."

"Certainly."

I led the way back to the office and partially closed the door. "There was an animal nailed to the front door."

Her hand flew to her mouth.

"Along with a letter suggesting we leave town." I sat down on the chair next to Mom and grabbed her hand. "Mom, do you want to leave town?"

She snorted. "Not like this." She thought a second. "I think we need a vacation. But," she held up a finger, "not until these problems are resolved."

Problems. Murder, slaughter, men trying to take over the company, my ex-boyfriend stalking me, Sam actually talking to me, cats and dogs sleeping together, and who knows all what. I started giggling.

"Are you all right?" Mom said, concerned.

"No," I said. "But then again, I've never actually

been all right. Why did you come by?"

"The vet said that we could pick up Josie today. I was wondering if you had a preference in what kind of cat things I get."

"You don't need me for that."

"Well, no," she said. "But I would like you to be home when Josie comes."

I sat back in my chair. "Mom, I'm wondering if we can board Josie there a little bit longer. These animal slaughters have me a little freaked out. I think we should leave her at the vet with strict instructions not to let her be picked up by anyone other than you or me."

Mom nodded. "I'll go right there."

"Then, if someone does try to pick her up, we'll have an idea who's been sending these threats."

"Okay." Mom hesitated. "You think somebody would pay for a cat just to kill it?"

I sighed. "I don't know quite what to think, frankly."

I heard a knock on the door. "Yes?"

The door opened slightly, and Reed stuck his face in. "Is there anything else?"

"No."

He slipped in and closed the door. "You know, it was very stupid of Cody to rip the letter off the door. He strikes me as a bit smarter than that."

"So?" Mom said.

I got his drift. "And you're thinking that Cody did the threatening letter?" I rolled my eyes. "Honestly, you have a bug in your bonnet about him."

"I told you," he said. "He has a record. He's at the top of my list."

"Well, rearrange your list!"

"If we used your list," he said. "Your ex-boyfriend Vince would be on the top of it."

"Yeah, well, why don't you look at his record?"

175

Mom looked back and forth at us like we were at a tennis match and she was the line judge.

"I did," he said.

"And..."

"Two previous charges for stalking, but that's it."

"So—he's upped his game."

Reed shook his head. "No. I talked to him. He swears up and down he wouldn't hurt animals, and I believe him."

"I'm supposed to trust your belief?"

"Well, you might consider," his voice was rising, then he stopped a moment, and his voice went back down to a low tone... "you might consider that when this last incident happened, he was in jail."

"What about—" I pointed at his pocket, "that?"

"He didn't get glue, magazines or newspapers in jail, and he certainly didn't tack that up."

"Why not?"

"For one thing, he would have needed hammer, nails, and something to shoot out the streetlight."

"And why couldn't he have done that overnight?"

"I went through his possessions. He barely had a comb and a toothbrush." He held up his hand. "And for another thing, he was sent back to Detroit last night, in the care of another police officer. Seems he had a previous charge outstanding."

"Bastard," Mom said. We both looked at her.

"Well," she said, "I didn't like him, either."

"I know, Mom."

The fact was that since I knew it wasn't Vince, I had no other viable suspects. Our contractors were a varied sort, but I didn't think they would be violent. Mike Collingsworth, quite frankly, hadn't bugged me since the funeral. I supposed he could be behind these attacks, but it—oh, I don't know, because I didn't know him—it just didn't seem to be his style. I saw the man as more direct than that.

It could be anyone in town., and this frightened me. Hell, as far as I knew, it could be Mrs. Grundy from church. Maybe Ashley Weedman didn't like the way I mentored her in her labs, and that sweet sad exterior held a ravenous killer. Maybe Mrs. Grant tortured animals for fun and profit.

Yeah, I was getting a little silly. And punchy.

I picked my purse out of the drawer. "Hey," I said, "how do I know that all these problems didn't come from you? I know very little about you, except what I've been told." I had palmed the pepper spray canister.

Mom turned to me. "Carrie. Don't be ridiculous."

"I'm not ridiculous. Who better to commit a murder than one who was supposed to stop a murder?"

"Are you accusing me of murdering Joe?"

Just then, it occurred to me that accusing and threatening a man — a police detective! — in a closed room with nothing for defense except for a small can of pepper spray was not the wisest thing to do. Oh, well—what was the saying? "In for a penny, in for a pound?"

I had a lion in a den, and I hoped that the lion would blink and started purring.

"Yes." I said, resolute.

He started laughing. "You've been reading too many bad detective stories, Miss Burton."

I started to relax, then tensed up again, then relaxed again. "You're right," I said. "That was dumb of me."

Wisely, he stayed silent.

"I had forgotten that you were having Thanksgiving dinner with us when the animals were placed on our porch."

He looked nonplussed. I think he had expected me to say that of course, I couldn't suspect him, his character was beyond reproach, yada, yada. But, the fact was, I still didn't know him that well, so why not suspect him?

"I think," he finally said, "that I had better get these

back to the station so that this can be sent out to a lab."

"You don't have one in the station?" I said.

He grinned. "Now I know you've been watching too many CSIs." He started to leave.

"Detective," Mom said.

"Yes, ma'am."

"Carrie's under a great bit of strain right now. Please don't hold this against her."

"Mom!"

Reed nodded. "I would have thought the same thing in her place," he told her, then he slipped out the door.

"Mom."

"Carrie."

"Don't apologize for me."

"I wasn't," Mom said, which was true, sorry never came up in the conversation. "I was explaining."

True. But there was a part of me that wanted to remain strong in front of Reed. I'm not sure why. I wasn't sure I could explain it to myself. I guess it was because I knew he was a strong sort of man—he had to be, to survive the murders of his family—and I wanted to prove I could stand up before him, equal to him, rather than collapsing in his arms like a mewling kitten like Josie. Like I had before.

Even though that sounded good, too.

I put that thought out of my head.

"Anyway," Mom said, continuing as if we hadn't been interrupted, "I'll tell the vet to keep Josie for as long as possible. We'll pay for it."

"Of course. As long as I get visitation rights."

Mom smiled. "Of course." She got up, then sat back down.

"What?"

"I think that now's the time to tell you something you don't want to hear."

"And what's that?"

"I think you should take Andy out after this — un-pleasantness — is over."

I blinked. "What do you mean?"

"A date, I mean."

I gaped at Mom. "Are you kidding, Mom? I'm not going to ask the man who thought I was a suspect for murder for dinner."

She shrugged. "Why not? You've already eaten with him once."

"Because you asked him to Thanksgiving dinner."

"So?"

"I'm not going to ask..."

Ted stuck his head in the open door. "Bad timing?" he said.

"Good timing." I said.

"Maybe you can talk some sense into her about Andy." Mom said, passing Ted by.

"I doubt it," Ted said.

I rolled my eyes.

CHAPTER 17

Detective Reed came up into my office a week later. "I would like to examine the crime scene again," he said, without preamble.

I looked up from my paperwork. "It's been quite a while, I said. "Are you sure that the cats and the raccoons haven't messed it up for you?" Actually, I wanted to see it again, too.

"Have you seen many cats around here again?"

I frowned. "Sadly, no."

"And have any humans been down there?"

"Not that I know of," I said. "Actually, I had it locked up, and I have the only key."

"So—may I?" He looked as if he wanted to say "May I, Mother?" but refrained at the last moment.

"You may, as long as you stop making unfounded accusations. Like accusing Cody." I laid my pen down. "So, did you find anything on the letter?"

"No." He was silent. But his blue eyes were fixed on me.

"I'll go out with you." I had wanted to see the scene, but I hadn't authorized anybody to lift the trap door. I was afraid of contamination of any crime scene, although the guys told me that any cats or raccoons probably had swarmed back in by now, in spite of us not seeing any.

I got up and shrugged on my coat. I had broken down and gotten one of those tough canvas coats. I figured if I was going to be wandering around the yard, my stylish down coat wasn't going to do.

We walked out into the yard. The day was clear and cold and all together a relatively typical early December day. Some leaves blew past, driven by a hard wind. I shivered. I was going out and viewing a murder scene, and the cold weather was just the scene to view a murder. I shivered again.

We reached the building. The door was wide open; we keep the doors open during the day, no matter the weather. I unlocked the trap door. Reed pulled it up, then pulled out his flashlight. He gave me a look, then lowered himself into the opening. He flashed the light around, and I grabbed the light out of my pocket, flashing it around. One thing became completely obvious to me.

"He wasn't murdered here, was he?" I said. "No blood."

Reed sighed. "No. He wasn't. He died someplace else."

"Have you figured out where?"

"Not yet."

"But why bring him here?" I mused. "Why kill him and bring the body here?"

He crept to the corner where Joe's body had lain. "I just wanted to see if there was something left. "

I carefully lowered myself down into the hole. I would need help getting out, I could tell, but I had to know what was down there. I very carefully stepped where Reed had landed so that I wouldn't be accused of tampering with evidence.

I flashed my light around. The ground was literally dirt. Over by the openings, I could see some dead grass. Up above were some ancient pipes—I remembered that Dad had told me that this was used as an office building at one point. The spiders had gotten a good foothold under here. I shrugged. I wasn't bothered much by spiders; I let them be, they let me be. I wasn't too fond of spider webs in my hair before, though.

I had never been down here before, and, if Joe hadn't been taken here, I would never be here again. I could see cat feces in one corner, made a face, and looked another direction. I went past another spot, then put the light back. I looked above that spot—no, no knothole. "Detective, look over here."

He glanced up. "They're a bunch of cigarette butts."

"Yeah, but why? They didn't put them through a knothole; there are none over there."

"Why would anybody crawl under here to dump a bunch of cigarette butts?"

"Exactly." I looked at the floor above me. "It's suicide to have a cigarette around here. This building would go up in flames in a moment."

"Don't you have fire suppressors here?"

I laughed. "A small place like this?" I swept the light around some more. "There's a trowel over there."

"It's ancient," Reed said. "I just figured that somebody dropped it down here accidentally and never bothered to pick it up."

"Possible."

"You see anything else?" His voice was this side of mocking.

I felt a little burst of anger. "Not me. What about *you*, detective?"

"Not a thing." He sighed. "Real life is certainly not like CSI."

"No." I looked over at him. Did he just admit a weakness?

"I always wanted to be Quincy," he said. "But I didn't want to be a doctor."

I snorted. "Did you think you would get medical training by osmosis?"

He didn't answer. Sharing time was over, I guess. I decided to go over by the trowel. Something about it bothered me. "Why bring a trowel down here?"

"I don't know."

"Can I pick it up?"

"You have gloves on?"

I shrugged them out of my pocket. "Yes."

"Be very careful."

I lifted it off the ground and brought it close to my flashlight. "It has fresh dirt on it."

"How can you tell?"

I blinked. He was right. I couldn't tell fresh dirt from old dirt. Still, it implies that it was used for digging, and recently.

I looked around. "Detective," I said, looking at the ground, "I believe that the ground has been dug up over here."

Reed was puttering around in a corner. "How can you tell?"

I squatted down. "Because I see a handprint. It looks like it might have pushed down on loose soil."

"Don't touch it."

"Wasn't planning on it." I looked up. "Do you need some plaster for a cast?"

He grunted. "I'll call for some of our special plaster."

I inclined my head. "I'll keep people out of my hole."

Reed started to grin.

"Shut up." Right now, I really didn't like Detective Stetson Reed.

An hour later, Reed was back with his special plaster. I wandered out to the yard with him, Ted looking on. "I'd rather," Reed said, "that nobody be down in the hole with me."

I looked up on the Internet what he was doing. He had mixed up the plaster, and, being very careful to what he was doing, poured it carefully into the impression. He looked around some more, then came up out of the hole.

"Don't you need to get it out?" I said, as we started walking back to the office.

Reed shrugged. "Takes at least thirty minutes to set. I'll be back. Can you keep people out of the building?"

184

I looked up at the clock. "Actually, fairly easily. It's quitting time."

Reed blinked. "I didn't realize that it was that late."

"Why don't you just stay here while it sets? My Mom's bringing supper in. Fried chicken."

"I shouldn't..."

"Well," I shrugged, "then you can watch me eat."

"I would suggest eating Mrs. Burton's fried chicken," Ted suggested. "I would stay around, but I need to get home to my wife."

"But...?"

"Is my mother a suspect?"

"Right now," Reed said, "everyone is a suspect."

Ted grinned. "I doubt that Mrs. Burton is one of your high up suspects. You can eat her supper without re-percussions."

"Cody and one of his buddies are helping me move some office furniture around," I said. "Supper is their brib-ery." I saw Mom out the window. "There's Mom right now. Might as well sit down."

"I'll pass, thanks."

"Your loss." Mom came in the door, and the chicken scent wafted through the office. I don't know what Mom does to the chicken to make it taste so good, but I once tried to recreate her recipe. No go.

I could see Detective Reed salivating in the corner, but his pride was never going to allow him to take any chicken. I jerked with my head to Mom, and she glanced over. Then she put a leg and a breast on a plate, put in a dollop of mashed potatoes, a few beans, and some plastic cutlery and walked it over to the Detective. She placed the plate in front of him, then stood back. "Don't insult my cooking," she said. "You've had enough of it in church."

His face relaxed and he grinned involuntarily. "Too true, Mrs. Burton. Marie."

"It occurs to me," Mom said, "that it must be hard

to be a detective in one's hometown."

"It's not like our crime rate is high," Reed said. "Usually, I get loaned out to other cities."

"Ah," she said. "Are there any interesting stories you could tell us?"

"Well, there may be one story I can tell you."

My Mom. I think she could talk to a pet rock and get it to open up like a rose. "If it doesn't compromise security or any such thing," she said.

"As long as I keep names out of it, I can say things," Reed said.

"So," I said, "a year down the line, you can talk about this case and get away with it?"

Mom gave me a dirty look. I shut my mouth with a snap, then muttered. "I'm sorry. That was a low blow."

"It's all right," Reed said. "Probably in a year, you'll have more rumors than fact around this place. I'm sure you would rather have truth than half truths."

"Depends on the truths," Cody said. He stared at Reed; I don't think he had quite forgiven him for calling him a felon.

We ate the rest of supper in silence. "Well," Mom said. "I'll listen to your story later. I have a card game at Mrs. Gates's house." She got up and I helped her pack up the dishes. "Don't be too late."

"Thanks, Mom, for supper," I said. "I'll see you later." I saw her out the door, then turned to Cody and Reed.

I sat in one of the office chairs. "Cody, we were speculating on why somebody would dump old Joe in our building." I turned to Reed. "You know, something occurs to me. Were you certain those wounds were fresh?"

"I still need the report from the M.E.," he said. "But I'm reasonably sure."

"But you're not one hundred percent," I said.

"True," he said. "I don't see a lot of murders."

186

"So, if the wounds were partially healed, he wouldn't be bleeding in that hole."

"Well, no," he said, "I suppose not."

"Which could mean that he climbed into the hole by himself and either got confused or just plain old died down there."

Reed sighed. "He was definitely beaten. At his age, a beating like that could kill him. I'm just not sure of the timeline."

"Hmmm. I wonder if he had buried something in that hole."

"Or something," Reed said, "was buried there before and he was digging it up."

"Who owned the lumberyard before Dad?" I asked.

"It was an old couple named—Mulligan," Reed said. "They were going to retire to Florida. But the Newton family owned that barn first."

I opened my eyes wide. "So if something was buried there, it's a possibility that Joe would know about it."

"Or," Reed said, "would have known about it before he went to the War. Afterwards, after his mind had been messed up, who knows?"

"Maybe he had a moment of clarity," I mused.

"Possible."

"All speculation," Reed said. "I hate speculation. I like to deal in facts."

"Whereas I deal in speculation almost every day," I muttered.

"And you're learning to deal in speculation in the real world."

"What are you talking about?" Cody said.

"I like to write fiction," I said to the counter.

"Yeah?" Cody said.

"Yeah. Like fantasy and science fiction stuff."

"And I like to read that stuff," Reed said. I looked up. "I usually have two or three books from the library."

"You do?" Cody said.

Reed shrugged. "It's pretty cool."

I pointed at him. "So why do *you* read it?"

"Escapism." He blushed.

Cody looked from one to the other. "You two have something in common?"

I glanced at Reed. "That is kind of odd."

"I know it is," Reed said. He glanced at his watch. "Another few minutes."

"So," Cody said. "What do you think you'll find?"

Reed looked sharply at Cody. "I'm not sure. The identity of the killer, perhaps."

"Really," Cody said, looking incredulous. "You can find it from plaster?"

"Sometimes," Reed said, seemingly casual, but I could see tension in his hands. His hands were out of sight from Cody.

He still suspected Cody. Well, I would let him play this out. I still thought Cody was innocent of everything, but...

I had a flip of mind, if that makes any sense. Using my creative mind, I suddenly saw all of the events from Reed's point of view. And, from Reed's point of view, the whole thing made sense. Cody, coming from California to an uncle who was trying to gain control of the lumberyard. Cody, voluntarily leaving Southern California, where he had lived all of his life, to Southern Michigan—a far different climate, especially this time of year. Not that that was suspicious in itself, I told myself, maybe he just wanted to come to Midwestern values and get away from what I supposed was a wild California scene.

But then there was the car theft. I have to admit that was pretty stupid, but Cody had explained it away as youthful indiscretion. Possible. Had Reed found anything else? I didn't know. I didn't think so. I met Reed's eyes. Suddenly, I knew that the car theft wasn't the only thing.

"Cody," Reed said, easing his arm to a different position, "one thing I found in my investigation was that a whole bunch of dead animals were found in your old neighborhood.

Cody stood wide-eyed. "Do you think that *I* killed animals?"

"I think it's a tremendous coincidence." With one hand, he took a bite of chicken wing, the other one floated around his waistline.

"Have you found other murdered animals around here?" Cody said. "I mean, before these last few weeks?"

"No, but I dare say that anyone who would do such a thing would find some good woods around here to bury his obsession in."

Damn it, Reed was making too much sense.

He looked at his watch. "The plaster should be set by now. Carrie, would you like to join me?"

"Cody," I said, "when is your friend showing up?"

He looked at his watch, seemingly casual. "Should be in about five minutes or so."

"Okay. We'll be in shortly."

"Are you going to lock the yard gate?" Cody said.

I frowned. "I don't see the point. We'll just close it so that customers won't drive in."

Cody smiled. "Okay."

Reed motioned to me, and I put on my coat. We exited the office. I could see the tension in his back and hoped in a couple of different ways that Cody did not.

As soon as we cleared the door, I said, in an undertone, "You baited him."

"I did," Reed agreed. "If he's truly innocent, as you believe, then nothing will happen."

"And, if he's guilty of murder?"

Reed was silent for a second. "I wish you weren't here. I'm sorry I drew you into this. I'm truly hoping that he's not a murderer."

We walked into barn number three. I felt as if I were hyper-alert. I wanted to glance back toward the office, yet I didn't, so I looked around at the barn as if I were seeing it for the first time.

I had known it was old, but I guess I had never realized how old. Most of the buildings in our yard were pole barns; this was the only stick built. Part of the barn floor was made of two by sixes, and it seemed retrofitted to the walls. The section of floor with the trap door was part of this.

The floor creaked ominously as we walked across it. The few times I had been in this barn I had wondered how safe the boards were and whether I was going to fall through the floor.

Even though the day was cold, I could see the dust floating in the stray rays of sunshine coming in the windows. I looked at Reed. He glanced back, then motioned me around so that I faced the door. He then pulled up the door and glanced into the hole. "I should make you go down there," he murmured, "so that my hands are free."

I was going to tell him that he was being paranoid, but I couldn't. He climbed down into the hole, then I thought, well—and dropped down beside him. The gardening trowel down there bothered me. "Detective Reed?" I said.

He was carefully pulling up the plaster. "Yes?"

"May I dig under the plaster?"

He smiled. "My thoughts, exactly." He handed me the trowel. "Be very careful."

I had dug only three inches down when I hit something. I felt a little like Indiana Jones. I looked up at Reed, then he handed me a plastic bag. I used the side of my hand in the bag to clear it off, then I pulled it out.

A small gold bar.

My eyebrows rose as I thought about the last thing I heard Joe say: "Thar's gold in them there hills!"

190

How sad. He knew what he was talking about. Why the Newton family buried gold under the barn, I didn't know, and I didn't care, but it looked like Joe got murdered for it.

I looked at Reed. He pointed up.

"Damn," I said.

Mike Collingsworth was standing at the top of the door with a gun. Pointed at me. I blinked. Of all the things I had never thought would happen, this was happening to me. I've only had a few of those kinds of things happen in my life. One was riding on the outside of a San Francisco Cable Car. Another was seeing Hilton Head in Hawaii. A third was driving in the front car of a monorail at Disney World.

This one was the weirdest.

"Why?" I said.

"Joe Newton was my uncle," he said, simply. "My mother and her family chose never to acknowledge him, but we always knew he was rich. So when my far-off cousin came to me with a story his mother told him..." Cody moved into view.

"Cody," I said, not surprised. I guess Reed had me convinced more than I thought. "I would ask why, but I guess I know."

He shrugged.

"What I don't understand is why you just didn't bide your time and dig up the bars on your own time," Reed said.

I smiled. "Because he didn't know where they were. May I speculate?"

"Do," he said. "Or do not."

Gads. We were being held at knifepoint, and Reed was quoting Yoda.

"So," I said to Cody. "Your mother was Joe's... daughter?"

"Granddaughter," he said. "Grandma was getting

old and senile when she *finally* told us about her father and her mother. Things were getting a little sticky back home."

"Meaning someone was onto you about the animal torturing?"

"They were just animals," he whined. "Not like they have feelings."

"Yeah, like you would know."

"Carrie," Reed whispered. "Don't argue with a sociopath."

"So," I continued. "You came back here to meet good old gramps, and he wasn't quite what you expected."

"No," Cody said. "I was rather disappointed. I was kinda expecting this rich dude, from the way Great Grandma talked, and found this crazy old coot."

"So when did you start taking him seriously?"

"Grandma said that she started babbling about gold she had seen. But she didn't know where it was. When I said something about gold to Joe, he started talking about gold in the hills and he would always look at this barn."

"So," I said, "you thought he knew more than he was saying?"

"I tried to get it out of him," Cody growled, "but he wasn't cooperating, then suddenly he was dead."

Suddenly? The man was stabbed to death. What could be sudden about that?

"I was in the office alone; I wasn't sure where to dump the body, so I put him in a sack, wheeled him across the railroad tracks, and put him under building number three until I could move him out to the woods."

Here alone? Here? Joe was murdered in the office? I never saw any blood! He must have cleaned it up so thoroughly that we never saw anything.

Of course, it sounded as if he had a lot of practice.

"But you never found the treasure," Reed said.

"Do you have any idea where it's from?" I said.

"Investments." Collingsworth said. "The Newtons

had a fear of banks."

"The Depression?"

Mike shook his head. "Apparently from one of the Panics long before the depression."

It finally occurred to me that we weren't going to get out of this alive.

Mike shook his head.

"Don't kill us," I said.

Reed was silent.

"If only your mother had sold the yard to me." Mike shook his head again. "I don't want to kill you."

But I could see the look in Cody's eyes. *He* wanted to kill us. It was chilling.

"Then don't kill us," Reed said.

A shadow came across the floor. "Then I suggest you don't, either."

"Mom!" She was holding an old hunting gun. Dad's gun. I never knew she knew how to load it.

"Back away from my daughter."

"I don't think so." He looked at the gun. "That gun has to be at least forty years old. Do you even know how to load it?"

"My husband taught me." She cocked the trigger. "So yes," Mom said, "I know how to load it."

He started looking more concerned. "Still," he said. "We have a stalemate. I can shoot your daughter faster than you can shoot me. And—we're two against one."

A shadow came in behind Mom. Oh, God. This day was just getting better and better.

Vince.

"I thought you had him driven back to Detroit," I murmured.

"I had," Reed said. "But I couldn't make him stay there."

I shook my head. "I just wish I knew what side he was on."

He caught sight of the gold, still in my hands. "Is that—gold?"

"Yes," Mike said, "it is. Who are you?"

"I'm Carrie's..." he looked at the gun, then looked at my Mom. "Carrie's..." He stopped. "Gold, huh?"

"Yeah," Cody said.

He made a sudden move and grabbed the gun out of my Mom's hands. He then pushed her back towards our hole. "How much will you pay me to remain quiet?"

"Vince!" I said, shocked.

He glanced over at me. "How much?"

"Shoot him," Cody said. "Or give him to me. I can experiment on him."

"Experiment?" Vince said. He didn't look so certain anymore.

"Vince, you really don't want him to experiment on you," I said. "Unless you don't value having your skin on your body."

He swung the gun to cover both Mike, Cody, and us. I'm not entirely sure what he was thinking.

"Reed," Mike said, "throw out your gun or else your girlfriend gets it."

Reed looked at me. "Trust me," he muttered as he slowly leaned over to get his gun. It seemed to take an inordinate amount of time, then he got it loose. He straightened up. "No," he said, pointing the gun at them. "You are all under arrest."

Mike turned at Cody and grinned. "You and what army?"

Six policemen poured into the barn. I hadn't known that there were that many policemen in Herculaneum—oh, but some of them were with the Sheriff's office. "That army," Reed said.

"Lay down your weapons," one of them said.

In the background, I saw Sam Kline hovering. Had he called the police?

"How did you know?" Reed said to Officer Cole.

He hitched a thumb. "Kline called us. Why were you here without backup?" He watched Cody, Mike, and Vince being escorted out of the barn, then turned to us, giving us a helping hand out of the hole. Mom was leaning against the saw table, looking as if she were going to faint any second.

Reed relaxed. "I didn't think that things would progress quite this far. And I wasn't sure that Cody was our prime suspect, until he and Mike made their move." He shook his head. "Stupid, I know. I'm sorry, Miss Burton."

"I think, under the circumstances, you can call me Carrie," I said, laying a hand on his arm.

He grinned. "I wouldn't presume."

"As long as I can call you—Reed." I said, smiling broadly.

He turned to me, and I looked him in the eye. My smile dropped as I searched his face. I think he actually did like me, and, in spite of myself, I actually liked him. I pecked the side of his face, then he turned his head, and we actually met, lip to lip.

It was... nice.

It only seemed to last a moment, but then Mom cleared her throat. "Um," she said, "I think if you're going to do much more than that, you may not want an audience."

We looked around. Cole was grinning broadly, Sam looked stunned, and Mom looked amused. "Maybe we should go into the office, Detective Stetson Reed," I said primly, my face flushing, but when I looked at him, my mouth turned to a grin.

"So," I said, as we walked to the office. "What's going to happen to the gold?" We had waited in the barn until all that seemed to be there was dug up. Sam was waiting for us in the office.

"Well," Reed—Andy! -- said, "I'm not a lawyer,

195

but since it was found on your land, I suppose some of it could be yours. After all, there's not exactly a note of ownership. Just hear-say."

Mom was walking beside us. I glanced at her, and she shook her head. "I think that it should belong to the Newton family. Were there any other family besides Cody and Michael?"

Andy shook his head. "We'll have to search, but I didn't find anybody when I searched. We could ask those two, but I don't trust either one to tell the truth anymore."

I closed my eyes. "I thought I was a better judge of character than that. How could Cody fool us all for so long?"

"He fooled your Dad, too. And Ted. Your Dad only had praises for him."

"Sometimes sociopaths are great actors."

"Do they know good from evil?"

He shook his head. "Not from what I've heard. They're habitual liars, too."

"Oh, good," I said, "I've been surrounded by sociopaths and psychopaths. Maybe I can find another personality disorder to add to my collection."

Reed smiled. "If I may suggest..."

"You know of another personality disorder?" I stared at him. He grinned back at me.

"Well, I was wondering," he stopped short and glanced at my Mom, who nodded. "I was wondering if we might discuss that over dinner sometime."

"Preferably with me," Mom added. "At least for that discussion."

I glanced at Mom. "Why, Detective. Are you asking me out on a date?"

"Um," he looked at the ceiling. "Um, yeah, I think I am."

"Well," I teased, "I'm not sure. Are you trustworthy?"

"Perhaps we'll need to go on a date so you can find out."

"Well—okay." I feigned reluctance, but I smiled to remove the sting. "But we're bypassing what I asked in the first place. What will happen to the gold if we can't find any of Joe's relation? He must be related to someone."

"Actually, believe it or not, Joe has a will," Reed said.

I blinked. "He does?"

"The Grants were in possession of it. It was dated June of 1942, before he went to war."

"What did it say?"

"Any money or possessions were to go to his wife and child first. In the event of their death, it was to go to his parents. In the event of their death, it was to go to a charitable organization." He paused. "Sometime later, the Grants made a revision that any of Joe's possessions were to go to the foster care home."

I smiled. "That means that Ashley will have whatever she wants."

"I suppose," Reed said. "I think I would suggest a trust."

I shrugged. "That might help." I sighed. "We can think about that later."

"So," I said, as we walked into the office. "What now?"

"I suggest," Reed said, "that we have supper."

I blinked. "The date, already?"

"No," Mom said. "Tonight, we're going to celebrate."

I smiled at Andy, at Sam, and at Mom. For now, all was right with the world. I looked up at the heavens. "Thanks, Dad," I said. "I think we're going to be fine."

"You bet we are," Mom smiled. "Now, let's go— and Sam, too, for calling the police. Andy?"

"I think my bosses won't find it out of line if I ask a

few more questions," he said.

"Sam?"

He looked at the ground. It looked as if he were about to refuse, then he looked up. "Okay."

Andy smiled at me. For the first time in a couple of months, I looked forward to the future with hope.

And now I could go pick up my kitten!

ABOUT THE AUTHOR

Lorraine J. Anderson has been experimenting with many kinds of fiction, including comic strips with the artist Sherlock, Fantasy stories, Science Fiction stories, fictional newspaper columns, Young Adult paranormal fiction and now, cozy mysteries. She hopes to someday make fiction more than a hobby. She is ruled over by three cats, Merlin, Muggle, and Miles.

For a full bibliography, go to www.lorrainejanderson.com.

Made in the USA
Monee, IL
21 November 2023

47073851R00109